Nymphomania

The Nymph Series Volume I

Ka'mooRe

KDP/Moore Blaque Entertainment

This novel is dedicated to all of my supporter and my freaks.
This one is for y'all, so let's get those freak flags flying!

I hope you enjoy reading this collection of short, erotic stories as much as I did writing them. Get yourself a glass of wine, light some candles, and let's get lost in the world of nymphomania. Don't be ashamed to let your freakiest desires come alive.

-Ka' mooRe.

Welcome to Nymphomania...

Nympho 1

Remember the Time

There comes a time in a woman's life where she realizes that she will no longer take the bullshit! I thought to myself, as I was packing my husband De' Vaughn's bags. I'm so tired of his cheating ass! I had the last straw when I found out he slept with one of my co-workers. The loud banging on the door interrupted my thoughts. When I heard the obnoxious yelling from outside, I knew exactly who it was.

"Monica, open the fucking door. I need to talk to you!" De' Vaughn yelled.

I took a deep breath. I knew this was going to turn into an argument.

"Why, De'Vaughn?" I asked. There was attitude laced in my tone.

"Because I pay for this fucking house! Now, open the got damn door 'fore I kick this shit in!"

He yelled his New Orleans accent growing thicker. His temper was rising by the minute. I slowly opened the door. I rolled my eyes as I watched him walk in and take a seat. I couldn't believe this smug muthafucka! He had an arrogance about him that told me he didn't think I'd do shit to make his life miserable.

"Look, Monica, baby. We can work through this bullshit. We have to let our kids know that no matter what, we're in this for the long haul," De'Vaughn said.

I pressed my lips together and rolled my eyes. This nigga was so full of shit. Whenever he got caught up with his extra-curricular hoes. He used our kids as an excuse. We sat in awkward silence. Despite me being mad at my husband, he was still the finest man in the world to me. Born and raised in New Orleans, he had the sexiest southern drawl. Every inch of 6'8" dark, smooth, chocolate man meat. He had these dark brown eyes that pierced my soul when he would look at me.

His deep waves made me seasick. His full lips always felt good on my kitty kat. His huge hands would palm my ass like basketballs. My man has a body to die for: nothing but muscle baby. What I loved most was his thick, long pipe; that would hit my spot and make me orgasm within seconds.

De'Vaughn ran his fingers across my face and asked, "What are you thinking about?"

I scooted closer to the edge of the couch. Being close to him was unnerving me, and I needed to stand my ground.

"Nothing, De' Vaughn. You need to go," I said.

This muthafucka smirked and said, "I ain't going nowhere until we talk."

He fanned his legs in and out to keep from getting hard. I swallowed the lump forming in my throat, but I wanted to be swallowing something else. I looked at him and knew he wanted nothing more than to fuck the shit out of me. Not just any old fucking, he wanted to punish me. He wanted to show me who was in charge. He wanted to tease and make me beg for that dick. He scooted closer to me and draped his arm over the couch and caressed my shoulder.

"I know that pussy wet," he whispered in my ear, while gripping my thigh.

He was so right. But I wasn't going to give him the satisfaction of knowing it. He was making my clit throb, as he circled my shoulder with his tongue.

I scooted away from him and said, "You said you wanted to talk, so start talking."

He smirked again. I hated that I was such a weak hoe; I was like putty in his hands. He started placing kisses on my neck and shoulder again.

"Monica, I miss you, and I love you. I just want to come back home," he said.

"You're a liar," I snapped.

He started laughing, and I didn't know what the fuck was so funny. Before I knew it, he picked me up and sat me on his lap.

"C'mon, don't be acting like that..." –he paused, pulling the straps of my shirt down— "You wanna know what I've been thinking about lately," he said.

He slowly ran his tongue across my nipples, causing me to arch my back. He kissed my neck and cheek, staring into my eyes, and moving my dark hair from my face and admiring my features. I'm sure at this moment he regretted cheating on me.

"You know what I have been thinking about?" he asked again.

Before I could ask what, he answered the question.

"The first time we fucked. Damn, it was so good. It was cute how you were playing hard to get. I'll never forget how you were taking my dick on that bench," De' Vaughn explained.

Although I was supposed to have an attitude, I laughed because I remember that night. The dick was better than I thought it would be. As he continued to kiss and suck on my neck and breast. My mind drifted back to the first time we fucked.

∞∞∞

1998...

De' Vaughn and I were attending Jackson State University, and both of us were the school's number 1 athletes. I ran track, and he played football. It wasn't unusual for us to be working out at the stadium late at night. He would either be practicing drills and routes while I would be working on my distance and endurance.

Tonight, something was different. I would always catch him eying me, and I heard from a few of my teammates that he had been feeling me. I ignored his advances because he was quite the whore on campus. I couldn't deny that he looked scrumptious! He had on a durag with a pair of compression pants; I knew the dick was big. He was shirtless as I watched him throw the football in the air and catch it.

I wanted to lick every single drop of sweat from his abs and chest. I tried to focus on my workouts, but he was a much-welcomed distraction. We made eye contact, and this man had my knees weak. I turned my back towards him as I continued with my stretching. About five minutes later, I could feel him behind me. I picked up my water bottle and took a slow, deliberate sip before turning to face him.

"How can I help you, sir?" I asked.

He smiled at me and said, "You were doing that wrong."

I laughed. He was referring to my hamstring stretches.

"What's the proper way to do it?" I asked.

He smirked and turned me around, so my back was facing him. His hard-on nestled into my lower back.

He ran his hands over my shoulders, grabbed my titties, and said, "I don't know why you're playing hard to get."

He kissed the top of my head. I smiled as he continued to caress my breast.

"Because you're a hoe," I said.

My eyes rolled to the back of my head as he kissed my neck and shoulder.

He pressed his lips to my ear and said, "If you quit playing games, this long, hard dick is all yours."

There was no doubt in my mind that I had creamed my panties. His strong hands caressed my stomach, and he used his left hand to slide inside my shorts. He used his right hand to wrap around my throat.

"Oh, my God! De' Vaughn, that feels so good," I moaned.

"Damn you are so wet," he groaned in my ear.

He turned my head so that we could finally kiss. We licked and sucked on each other's lips. He rolled my clit between his fingers. I could feel his dick grow harder as he continued to work my pussy.

"Baby, you're gonna make me cum," I moaned. He sucked my earlobe into his mouth.

"Not yet, boo, I want you creaming on my tongue," he whispered.

He slowly pulled his hand from my shorts. He bought his sticky fingers to my lips, and I gladly sucked my juices off. I finally turned around to face him. I couldn't deny how fine he is! He leaned down to kiss me and pulled my sports bra over my head. My perky breast swayed and bounced as my nipples grew harder. He used his big hands to grab my titties. He slowly circled my nipples, causing a tingling sensation to travel down my spine.

"I wanna taste you so bad, baby," he said, kissing my forehead.

"I wanna taste you," I said.

He smiled. I pressed my body closer to his, and I kissed his neck, gently biting his Adam's apple. I kissed his chest, licking and sucking on both his nipples.

"Fuck girl," he groaned.

I traced all 8 of his abs, finally making my way to my delicious treat. I got in a squat position and pulled his compression pants under his ass. His dick was so happy to be free that it bopped me in the forehead.

"Somebody looks happy to see me," I said, kissing the tip.

"Yeah, King Kobra, been waiting on you, baby," He said, looking down at me.

I slowly jacked him off as we stared at each other. I wrapped my lips around his juicy head as I lightly tugged on his balls. He let a long stream of spit fall, onto his shaft, and I eagerly gobbled him up. For the first few minutes, he let me do my thang. Once, he decided he had enough of me teasing him. He gripped the sides of my head and started fucking my throat.

"Monica, that mouth feels so good, baby. I know that pussy gone be fire. There you go, eat all that dick up," He growled.

I continued to suck and slurp him up; he tasted so good. I

wanted him to bust all in my mouth. I could feel my pussy grow wet-
ter as he slid in and out of my mouth. When he started dipping at the
knees, I knew he was about to nut.

"Got damn, fuck! You gone make me cum, baby!" he yelled.

Before I knew it, he was pushing me back and wrapping his
hand around his dick. I wiped my mouth and slowly got up. I pulled
my shorts off and started walking towards the bench.

"Monica, where are you going?" he asked.

I got in my favorite position, doggie style, and said, "Come take
this pussy nigga."

He happily obliged and ran over to me. He smacked both my ass
cheeks and started playing with my pussy again. He kneeled behind
me and slid his long tongue between the slick folds of my cunt.

"Oh, my Gawd!" I screamed as he sucked on my clit.

I was floating on a cloud.

"You taste so good, baby. I'm about to make this pussy mine,"
he groaned into me.

He alternated between eating my pussy and my ass. I was so
ready to take that dick.

"Give me that dick, boy," I growled.

He finally quit feasting on me and smacked my ass so hard; it
echoed throughout the stadium. He put his hand on my lower back to
push my arch deeper and slowly glided in me.

"There you go, baby. Let that pussy get used to daddy," he said.

His stroke started nice and slow, allowing me to get used to the
feel of him.

"Damn, Vaughn, you feel so good in me," I moaned.

He leaned down to kiss and suck the nape of my neck. My eyes were rolling to the back of my head. As I started to grow wetter, he started picking up the pace, giving me fast, deep strokes.

"You open now, boo. I'm about to fuck you the way I want, too," he growled.

"Yes, give me that dick boy. I want you to fuck me long and deep," I said back.

He smacked my ass again, causing me to cream all over his pipe. Although we were outside, our fucking and groans echoed throughout the stadium. I held onto the bench for dear life as he fucked me harder.

"Ooohh baby, you're going to make me cum! Keep fucking me just like that," I moaned.

"I want that sweet cream all over my dick. Where you want this nut?" He asked, sucking my earlobe.

"My pussy!" I yelled.

My body began to spasm and shake uncontrollably. "I got you, baby.

"I love how you, taking this dick. Fuck, I'm about to bust!" he yelled.

He held my hips tighter, and I could feel him releasing a heavy load inside my cunt. I leaned forward, causing him to pull out. I nearly lost my mind when he started eating me out. He made me come again. I was having an out-of-body experience.

He smacked my ass and said, "That pussy is better than I imagined."

I laughed and said, "That dick is on point."

He was still hard, and I was ready for round two.

"I want you to know, that pussy is mine now," he said, kissing my neck.

I nodded my head, agreeing with him. He picked me up, and I wrapped my legs around his waist. We shared another passionate kiss.

"Let's go back to my apartment, so I can see how sexy you look taking this dick," he said.

Once we got back to his place, we fucked all night long. I immediately fell in love with him and that dick.

Present...

"Monica, Monica! You good baby?" De' Vaughn asked.

I smiled and said seductively, "Come eat my pussy."

He had a big grin on his face as he picked me up and pulled my panties to the side. Little did he know, I was kicking him out and changing the locks after I got my nut. Payback was going to be a muthafucka!

Nympho 2

Day Dreaming

I imagine myself laying on a beach, with the sun beating down my titties and stomach. My legs are spread eagle as a, fine brown-skinned man, is down on his knees, feasting on me, as if I were a ripened mango. My juices slowly pour out of me, but he doesn't let one drop go to waste. I opened my eyes, only to be greeted by a long chocolate pipe hovering over my face. His dick bounces with excitement as it waits to enter my wet mouth.

Man number Two slowly bends at the knees and eases his steel into my throat. I begin to make slurping and popping sounds. The noises make number 1 eat my pussy faster. Even on my back, I can still deep throat a dick without gagging. The whispers of *Oh shit!* and *This pussy taste so good!* Made me grind and suck faster. I was being blessed with multiple orgasms.

Number Two pulled his dick out of my mouth and slapped it against my lips. I flicked my tongue across his juicy head. I started cumming as number Two released his load in my mouth. Number One traded places with Two, and another man straddled my stomach and slid his deliciously long dick in between my big titties. He toyed with my nipples as he titty-fucked me. I was floating on cloud nine.

All three of them stood up and asked in unison, "What's

your fantasy?"

I turned on my side and purred.

I bit my lip and said seductively, "To have all three of my holes fucked at the same time."

Their dicks bounced in excitement. Number Three decided he wanted to fuck my pussy, number Two wanted to fuck me in my ass, and number One enjoyed my mouth. We all got into our positions, and they entered my holes at the same time. The loudest gasp escaped my mouth. I welcomed this new experience. My pussy was being stretched in a delicious burn. Number Two pulled my head back so One could fuck my mouth deeper.

"You like having all three of your holes fucked?" One asked.

I moaned my answer as my eyes rolled to the back of my head. I pulled my bottom lip in and galloped on Three's dick, then I twerked my ass into Two's pelvis. One leaned over and spread my cheeks open, so two could dig deeper in my ass. Three was driving me crazy, sucking, and biting on my nipples.

Three and Two's strokes were going in unison, as One's dick push past my tonsils and fucked my throat deep. Spit was sliding down my chin and dripped onto Three's chest as he pumped faster in me.

"Oh my god! Y'all feel so good inside of me," I moaned.

"Damn, you got some good pussy baby," Three groaned.

"This ass is good boo," Two growled.

One could only mutter his responses about how good my throat felt. I was in pure ecstasy. My pussy and ass were being stretched blissfully, and my throat was getting stroked just the way I liked it too. When I felt my pussy tighten around Three's dick, I knew I was about to come.

"Ooh, baby, cream on this dick!" Three yelled.

Two pulled out of my ass and walked over to One, and they started jacking off. I was still galloping on Three's dick as my pussy muscles contracted violently.

"Oh, my fucking Gawd! I'm about to cum!" I yelled.

I felt my essence flow from my body. Me and Three shared a passionate kiss as he lifted up and joined the other two. I was on all fours, patiently awaiting my gooey treat. I took turns sucking their dicks and playing with their balls. I could feel each one of them tense up as they were preparing to nut. Before I knew it, Two yanked my head back as hot nut splashed on my face.

"Ooohh fuck!"

They yelled in unison as back-to-back orgasms showered us. Cum clung from my lips, nose, and lashes. Before they left, they all leaned down to kiss me. I was startled out of my sleep, by my annoying ass alarm. I was pissed that my dream wasn't a reality. My hands glided over my titties, and I gently pinched my nipples. I slid my fingers inside my panties and toyed with my clit, until I had another orgasm.

I wasn't the least bit surprised that I had soaked my panties and sheets. I laid in bed for a few more seconds. Hoping one day, my fantasy would cum true.

Nympho 3

Anywhere

There was nothing I loved more than the kinkiness of my marriage. We both enjoyed sex, especially in public places. It was the thrill of being caught or the look on other people's faces when they finally realized what was going on. My wife and I have done it in some pretty wild places; on the subway, restrooms, parking lots, restaurants right at the table, but nothing was gonna top what I had planned for her tonight.

My dick is getting brick, just thinking about it. I was lying in the bed naked, watching my wife get ready for her girls' night out. I licked my lips as I watched her get ready. She had on this short, skintight, snake-skin dress that left very little to the imagination. And I was trying my hardest to get her to slide down on my throbbing pipe before she left.

"Derek, if we decide to fuck now, we both know that I'm not going anywhere," she said.

I watched as she applied lip gloss to her full pouty lips. I began to stroke my dick as she shimmied into her thong.

"How long you plan on being out because I want some pussy," I said.

She grabbed her purse and keys.

She leaned over the bed , grabbed my dick and said, "I'll be back by one at the latest. Is that okay, daddy?"

Her smooth hand slid up and down my pipe. I nodded my head, letting her know that's cool. She leaned up and gave me a wet, juicy kiss. Then she abruptly stopped, smiled at me, and left out the room. I waited patiently until I heard her car pull out the driveway. I excitedly jumped off the bed and got dress.

∞∞∞

I handed security my VIP pass and walked into the club with all eyes on me. I didn't pay the lusty stares, or the green looks any attention. I walked into the club like I owned the place. The bouncer told me, there were two VIP sections left. I was trying to hurry up and find the one with the perfect view. I smiled once I found my booth. I had a bird's eye view of the dance floor. My area was perfectly secluded. I got situated on the velvet couch and waited for the bottle girl to come over. She finally approached the booth and looked around, confused.

"Hey, playa. Do you plan on inviting anybody up here with you?" she asked.

"Nah, not really; it's a private party. Don't worry, you gon' be taken care of tonight," I said.

"Aiight, what can I get for you?" She asked, popping her gum.

"Let me get two bottles of Ace of Spade and three bottles of Dussé," I said.

I looked up, and homegirl had a big smile on her face. I laughed as she walked off. I propped my feet up on the table and looked around the dance floor. I had one thing on my mind, and that was to find my wife. I bit my lip once I spotted her.

I watched as she bounced and shook that phat ass. Niggas were trying to grind up behind her. My grin grew bigger when I saw how she wasn't giving these niggas any play. I continued to watch as she got her groove on, teasing niggas and making bitches jealous. I was waiting for the perfect moment to get her attention. The bottle girl bought my drinks over, and I gave her $800. I popped the cork on The Ace of Spade and took a couple of sips. I walked over to the security guard and tapped his shoulder.

"What's up partna, you ready to invite some hoes in this bitch?" he asked.

I chuckled.

"Nah, she ain't a hoe. You see that fine ass woman right there?" I asked, pointing in my wife's direction.

"Shorty with the snakeskin dress and the phat ass," he answered.

I rolled my eyes and said, "Yeah nigga. That's my wife. I need you to bring her over here but don't tell her it's me."

"Aiight, I got you playa," he said giving me a pound.

I watched as homeboy walked into the sea of people. I watched as he approached the table with her girls. My wife stared the guard down, trying to give him attitude. He gently grabbed her arm and bought her over to my booth. When she realized it was me, she had a big smile on her face.

"I've been watching you all night, and I couldn't help but invite you to my private party. Do you have a man?" I asked, smiling.

"I'm married, but maybe I'm in the mood to have a little fun tonight," she answered seductively.

My dick started growing against my thigh.

"I got all the fun you need, baby. I liked how you were shaking that ass on the dance floor; you think I can get a private dance?" I asked, licking my lips.

She laughed as she watched me pull some money from my pocket.

"C'mon baby, I ain't gone touch you. Just a lil' dance for me," I said, flicking bills at her.

She slowly started winding her hips and grooving to the music. My dick grew harder as she lifted her leg and propped it up on the couch. The sweet smell of her pussy swam around me. When I tried to touch her, she slapped my hand away. She put her leg down, then turned her back towards me. She bent over, grabbing her ankles, giving me a peek of her ass cheeks and pussy. I was glad the D.J. decided to slow it down. It was setting the mood right for what was about to go down.

Something came over my wife because she started winding her hips like she was riding my dick. When *112's Anywhere* blared through the club, I was ready to turn this private dance into a private freak show. I got up and pulled her close so that she could feel my hard-on.

"No sex in the champagne room," she moaned.

I pressed my lips to her ear and started singing.

"We can make love in the bedroom, floatin' on top of my waterbed, I'm kissing you, running my fingers through your hair, In the hallway making our way beside the stairs, we can do it anywhere."

We were grinding on each other. I had my fingers in her mouth and my other hand between her legs.

"You ready for this dick?" I asked, licking her neck.

"I told you I'm married," she moaned.

I sucked her earlobe and said, "What ya' man don't know, won't hurt him."

We finally made our way to the couch as I took a seat. I watched as Tianna bent over again to show that pretty ass peeking from underneath her dress. I scooted to the edge of my seat and buried my face between her cheeks.

Tianna grabbed the back of my neck and moaned, "Oh my God! Derek, that feels so good."

I pulled her thong to the side so that I could slither my tongue towards her clit. I abruptly stopped when I knew she was about to cum.

"Let's do it anywhere," I sang as I got up and unzipped my pants.

My dick sprung outta my boxers as I entered her from the back. She continued to grab them ankles while my pipe throbbed inside of her. I pulled my bottom lip in as I began to stroke her creamy walls.

"Derek, you so feel good, daddy," she moaned.

I gripped her waist tighter to keep her from falling over. I had to get my stroke together because I wasn't ready for us to nut yet. I kept my gaze fixated on the crowd. My dick grew harder, wondering if people could see into our booth. I peeped, when security looked back, then faced the dance floor smirking. Tianna's moaning seemed to grow over the music.

"Oh my god! You are going to make me cum," she said, pressing her back into me.

I grabbed her neck and sucked her earlobe.

"You like when I beat it, baby?" I asked.

She nodded her head, letting me know she was loving my stroke. I blocked out the music blaring through the club and let the wet, smacking noises from our fucking become my music.

I pressed my face to hers and moaned, "Damn baby, you feel so good."

I noticed a group of guys walk by. I smirked as realization became their new expressions.

"Damn bruh, we need to be in this booth with you. I got next," the pack leader said excitedly. He was trying to walk up into my booth.

"Nah bruh, this is a private party," I said as I continued to blow Tianna's back out.

Tianna started laughing and moaned, "You are going to get us kicked out."

I kissed the nape of her neck and said, "No, I won't. We're good."

I got my balance together and got a good grip on her hips and started pounding away on her spot.

"Fuck daddy! You feel so good. That dick is so big," she yelled.

I could've sworn it sounded like she was shouting over the music. I started going harder; she dug her nails into my thighs. I could feel her slick juices begin to slide down me and her thighs. The neon lights made my wife look even more beautiful.

"Fuck me harder, Derek!" she yelled.

She started grinding into me and I grabbed her titties as my dick started throbbing inside her. I gave her a couple of quick pumps as her walls tightened around me, and we both came to-gether. Our moans and groans were muffled by the loud music and our kissing. I helped her pull her dress over her ass, and she helped me put my dick back in my pants. I fell back onto the couch and looked at my wife in amazement. She put her hands on my knees and leaned down to kiss me.

She gently bit my earlobe and whispered, "Let's go home so we can finish this private party. The last one home has to receive."

I watched as she switched out the booth and out of the club. I was giving her a head start because I wanted that pussy in my face.

Nympho 4

The Art of Fellatio

I believe that sucking dick and eating pussy is a form of art; it takes a special kind of person to do it. It has to come from the heart. You have to love the taste of your partner. The gaze they have in their eyes when they look down at you. Ladies, the way he softly runs his fingers through your hair when he's ready to fuck your throat. Fellas the way she pushes your head further into her crotch when you keep teasing.

I loved giving head, enjoyed it more than actually receiving it, but my husband has always made sure that I am satisfied. Right now, all I could think about was being on my knees, with my husband stroking his long, brown dick. My tongue patiently awaiting his thick gooey nut.

I slyly put my phone under the conference table and sent him a text; *"I'll have a naughty surprise for you, when I get home."*

I pressed the send button and waited for hubby to reply. I had completely zoned out of my meeting. I couldn't stop thinking about how bad I wanted him fucking my throat.

I looked down when my phone buzzed, and hubby texted, *"Dayum, I can't wait! My dick is hard already."*

I smiled as we continued to text back and forth. My swollen clit rubbed against my panties causing friction between my legs.

A gasp escaped my mouth.

"Is everything okay, Mrs. Collins?" My boss asked.

"Yes, everything is fine," I said.

I asked if I could excuse myself, and once my boss gave me the okay to leave, I headed to my office to get myself off.

Later that night...

I was standing in my closet, admiring myself in the full-length mirror. I was pleased with my look. I already had Tommy blindfolded, and his wrist and ankles tied to the bedpost. I knew he was impatiently awaiting his surprise. To make sure my baby busted a river load tonight, I started a petty little argument at the beginning of the week. Now I was about to relieve him of all the stress I caused. I grabbed my trick of the night off the night-stand and seductively walked out of my closet as if he could see me.

"Are you ready, daddy?" I purred.

"Hell, yeah, I've been ready. Baby is that a new perfume because you smell delicious," he said.

I looked down at my hand and smiled. Yeah, tonight was going to be magical. I walked over to our California king sleigh bed and kissed his feet, legs, and thighs. I purposely forgot about his dick that rested on his thigh. I licked and sucked on his hard stomach and nipples. I ran my tongue up and down both sides of his neck, then ran my tongue across his thick lips. I slowly pulled on his bottom lip and sucked his tongue.

He slid his tongue in my mouth and pulled on my lips. We kissed for about ten minutes, but now it was time to get this show on the road. I kissed my way between his legs, arched my back, and spread my legs. The smell of my wet pussy wafted around the room. Causing my eyes to roll to the back of my head. I lifted his dick and admired it.

My man had a beautiful dick; it was one color a cocoa brown, it was long with a slight curve to it, and it had the prettiest mushroom head. There was a thick vein that ran from his tip down to his base. As he was hardening, I slowly slid the grapefruit down his shaft.

"Dayum baby, you so wet!" He yelled.

I let the grapefruit sit there for a minute as I kissed my way up to the head. I sucked on it, to taste his sticky precum. I licked up and down his length. I let him slide down my gag less throat one time, so his pipe could get wet. I wrapped my hand tightly around the grapefruit and slowly moved it up and down his shaft.

"Oh, shit, baby. Why does it feel like you fucking and sucking me at the same time?" He asked.

I ignored him and kept my focus on the task at hand. I licked, sucked, and slurped all of his tasty meat, which was making my mouth wetter. If I moved my head one way, I made sure to move the grapefruit in the opposite direction. I kept my grip on the fruit and used my other hand to massage his heavy balls.

I slowly throated him, as spit glided out of my mouth and down my chin. I wrapped my lips around it and made a bobbing motion with my head. I could tell that Tommy was enjoying this, especially being tied up and blindfolded. As I continued to move the grapefruit up and down, I felt his body jerk serval times. Trying to break free. I quit sucking for a moment but continued to jack him off as I popped his swollen nuts in my mouth. I licked and kissed up and down his muscular thighs. Then I kissed his abs and chest again. I slid my tongue in between his lips.

"You want me to untie you, baby?" I whispered in his ear.

"Yes, I do, Naughtya! You are driving me fucking crazy," he growled.

I ignored his plea to be untied and went back to sucking. I extended my tongue out and let him fuck my mouth, rough and hard. Spit was now flowing out of my mouth as he pushed passed my tonsils. I closed my mouth around his pipe and began to suck it like my favorite lollipop. I wished Tommy could see my handiwork, but his jerking around and moaning let me know I was doing excellent. It was time to focus on the head; I pulled the grapefruit up so, it grazed the tip, and I swirled my tongue around it like an ice cream cone. I wiggled my tongue into his piss slit.

"Fuck, girl, this feels so good!" He yelled.

I went back to bobbing up and down his length. When I suctioned my jaws around his dick, his toes curled, and he thumped inside of my mouth.

"Shit, I think I'm about to cum," he growled.

I wasn't ready for him to cum yet, so I pressed down on his side vein. That way, he could fill my throat with his gooeyness. I sucked on his nuts as I continued to jack him off with the grapefruit. His balls became tighter as I kept working my magic. The fruit had just about run its course.

"Baby, c'mon please let me bust," he begged.

I let the fruit sit on his pelvis; as he slid deeper down my throat. I released his vein. Not long after that, he was thrashing against the headboard and releasing all of him in my mouth. It was so much of his delicious cream that it overflowed. I continued to suck to make sure not one drop went to waste.

I pulled the grapefruit from his shaft. Tommy's thick, curly patch of pubic hair was soaked with spit, cum, and fruit juices. My juices had soaked our 4500-dollar sheets. I climbed on top of him and sandwiched his semi hard-on between my fluffy cheeks. I put my ear to his chest to make sure he was still alive. I untied him, and he had this lazy look in his eyes and a crooked grin on his face. His cum still clung to my chin. As I leaned down to let him taste the fruits of my labor.

"Naughtya, baby, Imma get you back." Were his last words before he fell into a coma-like sleep.

Nympho 5

Every time

Have y'all ever had sex so good, that when you had a flashback, you had to quit everything you were doing to satisfy yourself? The dick was so good, that it had you strung out after the first taste. That's how I felt after I finally gotten me a taste of this fine chocolate masterpiece. His name's Terryll, and he stood at least 6′3″, had smooth milk chocolate skin, and these big hands that cupped my breast and palmed my ass so right. I had a thing for brothas with large hands.

Every time I saw Terryll, my panties would get so soaked that I had to wear a pantyliner, when I knew I would be around him. He was such a tease, and at times I knew he would lick those juicy lips to watch me quiver. We always passed each other in the stairwell or while I was getting my mail. He was a hood nigga, and lord knows, those were the type of men that made my pussy scream. My fingers stroked my clit faster, as I thought back to the first time we got our freak on.

∞ ∞ ∞

I was walking back from the corner store, trying to get into my apartment, before it rained.

"Yo, shorty, come here!"

I looked around to see who was calling after me. I saw Terryll stick his head out of his window and motion for me to come to him. I ran across the street, and he held the door open for me. As I took a seat in his decked-out ride, my eyes rolled to the back of my head. His car smelled just like him, intoxicating.

"How you been shorty?" he asked.

I loved his New York accent.

"I've been well," I said.

I watched as he lit his blunt and passed it to me.

"I'm okay," I said gently pushing his hand away.

"So, you a good girl, huh?" he asked.

"No, I just don't like it. I don't get high whenever I smoke," I explained.

"That's cause you ain't had no good shit..." –he paused, taking a deep puff– "Come here, let me show you something."

He pulled me close to him and blew smoke into my mouth. Our lips touched, and his tongue slid in my mouth. I quickly pulled away because my panties were becoming soaked.

"You ain't gotta be scared. You know I've been feeling you," he said, rubbing his strong hand up and down my thigh.

My nipples tightened and started poking through my tank top. He gave me the sexiest grin, and licked his lips.

"Them chocolate titties look like they ready to be sucked on," he said.

"They are," I whispered.

He leaned over and licked the top of my breasts. He sucked my nipples through my tank top and slid his hand between my legs. I let out a soft moan as his long slender fingers glided in and out of me.

"Oh, my Gawd! That feels so good," I moaned.

His tongue slithered up and down my neck. Then he sucked my earlobe into his mouth.

"I can't wait to feel you wrapped around my dick," he whispered.

I pulled his fingers from between my legs and licked my cream off.

"I want you to fuck me deep and hard," I moaned.

He slowly unzipped his shorts and pulled his boxers down. His chocolate pipe sprung up, hitting the steering wheel. He wrapped his hand around his dick and slowly stroked it. The raindrops falling on the windshield made me hornier.

"It's so pretty," I said.

He smiled and said, "C'mon and climb on it."

I pulled my shorts and tank top off and threw'em in the back seat. He moved his seat back as far as it could go. I climbed over the armrest and straddled his lap. I reached down and pushed his dick to the mouth of my pussy. Slowly sliding down all of his length.

"Ooh damn! You so wet," he moaned.

I sucked in a quick breath and pinched my nipples.

"Your dick feels so good," I said.

He leaned forward and sucked on my nipples. He tightly

gripped my bubble butt, and found his groove.

"Fuck Terryll, you so deep inside of me," I moaned.

He had a crooked grin on his face as he looked up at me.

"You got some good pussy," he said, sticking his tongue in my navel.

I cradled the back of his head as I feed him my chocolate breast. He licked his middle finger and then moved it in a circular motion on my engorged clit.

"Don't stop, Terryll! You feel so fucking good, boy," I yelled.

I watched him as he looked on in amazement as he slid in and out of me. And my cream started to coat his pipe.

"Dayum boo, you got a creamy pussy," he moaned, holding onto me tighter.

"You got some bomb dick."

My fingers pumped faster in me as I thought about how hard we came together.

"Ooh shit, I'm about to cum!" I yelled.

I slapped my clit as my essence started flowing out of me.

"Shit! That felt so good, daddy," I said.

He stood up from the foot of the bed, stroking his long pipe.

"Yo! That shit was hot as fuck. Now I'm ready to pipe that pretty thang out," Terryll said.

Whenever I think about our night together, I can't help but

have him between my thighs again.

Nympho 6

The Locker Room

The gym was my safe space. My oasis. My peace. It's where I come to clear my mind. Lately, working out hadn't been helping. I've been extremely horny, and not even a self-induced nut was satisfying. I've been coming to the gym damn near every day for the last two weeks to see if I could spot me some good ass. Nobody was up to my standards, which was kind of disappointing because I usually have some decent hook-ups here. I thought my luck had ran out until I spotted this fine ass, light-brown skinned dude checking me out. I recognized him, because he's also a regular.

He fit my criteria: tall, slim, and he gave off DL vibes. My dick was getting hard thinking about having his full lips wrapped around my pipe. For the next twenty minutes or so, we played this cat and mouse game. My eyes stayed fixated on him as he moved around the fitness center. Tonight, maybe homeboy's lucky night because I was in the mood to give some ass up. My eyes followed him as I watched him walk into the locker room.

I didn't want to come off like a creep or seem thirsty, so I waited about 15 minutes before making my way into the locker room. I finished my last reps on the weights and cleaned the bench off. I grabbed my towel and headed towards my destination.

When I walked into the locker room, I was surprised it wasn't packed. Then I remembered the gym was hosting their weekly basketball game. I walked over to my locker and grabbed my wash towel and body soap. I was hoping homeboy was still here. My dick was getting hard thinking about getting deep in him. I pulled my shorts and shirt off, then tossed them in my locker.

I wrapped my towel around my waist and headed for the shower. My ass not paying attention, walked into somebody and dropped my stuff. When I looked up, it was homeboy I had been watching. A smile crept on my face as he bent down to pick up my body wash and towel.

"Damn my bad, bruh. I didn't mean to knock your shit down," he said.

His deep voice was making me hard.

"You good bruh," I said, taking my belongings from him.

I let my hands linger on top of his for a moment. He looked at me and smiled.

"What's up with you? I peeped you checking me out on the floor," he said.

"I like what I see."

I craned my neck, so I could see what he was working with. I can't lie homie got a fatty.

"I'm Terry, by the way," he said, holding out his hand.

I took it in mine and said, "I'm Brandon."

We stared at each other, waiting to see who's going to make the next move. I watched as he ran his hands over my chest and abs, then pinched my nipples.

"You're making my dick hard," I whispered.

"I know, maybe we should get our thang started before niggas start pouring in here," he said.

I leaned into him, then pressed my lips to his neck and asked, "So you gone let me get in that ass?"

He smirked, "I got you."

Terry kissed my neck and unwrapped my towel from around my waist. He began jacking me off while we were kissing. I don't know if it was because I was backed up or what, but this had to be the best hand job I ever had. I ran my tongue across his thick lips, then pulled on his bottom lip. I sucked his earlobe into my mouth and played with his nipples. Terry positioned himself so he was standing in front of me, and we rubbed our dicks against each other.

"Fuck yo, this shit feels good," I moaned.

I spit in my hand. Then wrapped it around our ever-growing hard-ons. Terry leaned into me so we could kiss. He made a trail down my neck, chest, and abs. He made cool streaks along my thighs. He gently placed my balls in his mouth; he licked the underside of my dick before kissing the tip.

"Got damn boy," I moaned as he slid my whole meat down his throat.

I've experimented with women before, and I've gotten some good head, but there was nothing like getting head from a man. I loved the strong jawline and when their cheeks would cave in around my dick and how their strong hands would wrap around my shaft. The shit just felt amazing. I looked down, and Terry was in a squat position. Playing with his dick and bobbing up & down on my shaft.

"Damn, you taste good, B," he moaned, sucking on my head.

"Yeah, suck that dick, baby," I said.

I placed both my hands on the side of his head and started fucking his throat. His spit was gliding down my shaft and soaking my balls. I pulled my dick out and slapped it against his lips. Terry started sucking on my balls and licking my gooch. That was my hotspot and the quickest way to get me to bust.

"Hold up, yo, I ain't ready to nut yet. Get up against the wall," I said, lifting him up and pressing him against the wall.

"I hope you can eat ass good," he said.

I smiled because he was in for a real treat. I kissed the back of his neck and made a wet trail down his spine, then stopped at the crack of his ass. I placed kisses on both cheeks and smacked them. I palmed his ass like they were two basketballs and licked my lips at my delicious treat. I slowly kissed his hole, then circled my tongue around it. I slithered my tongue up and down his crack, making it sloppy.

"B, that tongue feels so good," he moaned.

"This ass tastes good," I moaned back.

I slid my index and middle finger into his hole to get him to open up. I knew this was going to be some good ass. The only thing that could be heard in the locker room was me sloppily eating ass and Terry's moans. He pushed my face further in between his cheeks and spit slid down my chin. I jacked him off as I shoved my tongue into him.

"C'mon nigga quit playing with me and give me that dick," he said.

I smiled cause he ain't said nothing but a word. I slowly stood up and kissed the back of his neck as I slowly entered him. Once I got the head in, I let out a loud gasp.

"Fuck yo!" I yelled.

I finally got all of me inside of him, and it felt damn good.

"That dick big man," he moaned.

"How you want it?" I asked, playing with my nipples.

"Fuck me fast and hard," he groaned.

I did just that. I spit in his hole to slide in and out more comfortably, and I started drilling his shit. Our moans and groans becoming louder. I didn't give a damn who saw or heard us.

"There you go nigga. Push that hole out," I moaned in his ear.

"Fuck daddy, you feel so good," he said, throwing that ass back.

Man, he felt heavenly, he was wet the way I like it, and that shit was starting to talk.

"You got some good ass, baby," I said, kissing his neck and ear.

"You got some good dick," he moaned.

I played with his nipples as I started hitting his spot, and he started going crazy. He reached underneath me and played with my balls.

"Fuck, boy, that feels good, yo," I groaned.

I could feel my nut building up. I wrapped my hands around the back of his neck and went deep. Our balls were smacking together. I slapped his ass, pulled out, and began to tip drill. I was trying my best not to nut.

"Damn B, you gone make me nut. I ain't never had no dick

this good," Terry moaned.

I smiled, "I might have to let you get this booty next. Where you want this nut?"

"Fuck, wherever you want to bust," he said. I continued to glide in and out of him.

"I'm about to cum!" he yelled.

No sooner had those words left his lips, he shot a thick stream of cum against the wall. My toes curled, I quickly pulled out and started jacking off. It was throbbing and wet from his cream. Terry got down on his knees and held his tongue out. Before I knew it, a thick wad splashed on Terry's face.

"Damn boy, that was good," I said.

"Hell yeah, I can't wait to get that ass next," he said.

I laughed and told him I got him. I leaned down to kiss him and taste my nut. Terry stood up and pinched my nipples. My dick started getting hard again. He grabbed one of my ass cheeks and started fingering me. The shit was feeling good. Before we could get 'round two popping, niggas began rushing into the locker room. We quickly ran into the showers and promised to hook up again.

Nympho 7

Speechless

My husband and I were enjoying our quality time. We were surrounded by burning candles and assorted colored roses: red, white, yellow, and black. We were enjoying our bath, and as I laid between his legs, he toyed with my erect nipples. Using a rose petal to glide over my silky skin.

"Baby, we needed this time away from the world," Ahmad whispered.

He kissed the side of my forehead. He was right; this last year and half had been draining on our marriage. We were ready to throw everything away.

"Ahmad, I love you so much, baby," I said.

"I love you too, Za'mani," he said.

He leaned down and fed me his thick, juicy tongue.

"Come on, let's get out the tub so we can make love," he said.

We both got out of the tub, dripping with water beads. As I dried my husband off, I slowly jacked him off. He gently pulled my hand away, so he could dry me off. He paid extra attention to my breast.

"Turn around so I can blindfold you." I happily obliged my

husband's request.

After he covered my eyes, he sandwiched his thick dick between my ass cheeks and guided me out the bathroom. He untied my blindfold, and my eyes wandered around the room. It was beautiful; there were candles everywhere, rose petals on the bed, two bottles of Ace of Spade on ice, and a bowl of strawberries and chocolate. I felt his dick start to grow and poke me in the back.

"Tonight, is all about you. I can't wait to feel you wrapped around my dick," he whispered.

I turned around and wrapped my arms around his neck and slipped my tongue in his mouth. He picked me up and wrapped my legs around his waist and gently laid me down on the bed. He kissed his way down to my navel and spread my legs open wider. He kissed the inside of my thighs, the back of my knees, sucked and licked on my calves. He kissed the arch of my left foot.

"Za' Mani, I want tonight to be all about you. Remember the first time we made love?" he asked, kissing my feet.

"Yes, I do," I moaned.

My husband was passionate and affectionate; he loved to make love to me. He kissed his way back up to me. Stopping at my pussy and swirling his tongue around my swollen clit.

"Oh my god! Ahmad, your tongue feels so good," I moaned.

He slowly kissed my navel, sucked on both my breast, and licked my neck. Then he fed me his pussy stained tongue. We kissed for what seemed like forever; he finally pulled away. Grabbed a bottle of Ace of Spade from the champagne bucket and popped the cork.

"Open your mouth, baby," he said gently.

I slowly opened my mouth, and he poured some champagne in until it overflowed. I swallowed and moaned as he licked the droplets that had glided down my chin and neck. He took another sip from the bottle and leaned back down between my legs. He opened my legs wider and flicked his tongue across my clit. Then he placed the cold bottle on my cunt, causing my clit to throb. He slowly moved the chilled drink around my pussy, making me cream. I shivered as he replaced the bottle with his thick tongue, against my swollen pearl.

"Damn, you taste so good, baby," he moaned into me.

"Your tongue feels so good," I said, pushing his face further into my snatch.

Luther Vandross was serenading the room as my husband continued to feast on me. Ahmad made love to my entire body. He licked whip cream from my toes. Kissed both of my cheeks and licked up & down my crack. Then he made his way back up to my breast.

"Hold your titties together," he said.

I leaned up and held my ta-ta's together and watched as he poured champagne into them. He greedily drunk it all up and gently bit my nipples. He held my face in his hands and kissed me. We took turns biting and sucking on each other's lips. Ahmad finally slid his hard dick inside me and kissed my neck.

"I love you so much, Za'mani. I don't ever wanna cause you any pain again," he whispered in my ear.

Tears started falling down my cheeks. He was pounding against my walls and breaking down all of my resistance. Everything that Ahmad and I had been through started to fade away with each stroke. My legs were wrapped tight around his waist as he dug deeper into my well.

"Ahmad, I love you so much," I moaned.

"I love you too, baby, and I'm sorry," he said.

I wrapped my arms around his neck and pushed his head further down, so we could kiss. He kissed my arms, as he opened my legs wider to go deeper. Beyoncé's *Speechless* was blaring through the speakers. Goosebumps popped up on my skin, my nipples became stiffer, and I grew wetter.

"Fuck! Baby, you feel so good inside me," I moaned.

His strokes became longer and more profound; my toes curled as my legs wrapped tighter around his waist. My eyes rolled to the back of my head, and I bit down on my lip.

"C'mon Za'mani, open them pretty eyes for daddy. Keep them eyes open while we cum together," he said.

His sweat dripped on my nose, and he pulled his bottom lip in. Just as Beyoncé was yelling, yes. My pussy muscles tightened around him.

He pumped harder and faster inside of me, "Fuck! I'm almost there, baby," he growled.

"Yes! Oh my god! Yes, yes, yes! Yeeeeeeeessssss, daddy!" I yelled.

I dug my nails into his back and bit down on his lip. He pumped his seed deep inside of me. As he stared deep into my eyes, we shared another passionate kiss as he continued to slowly grind into me.

"This will always be my pussy," he whispered filling me deep with his love.

Nympho 8

The Flight Attendant

I must admit that I had the perfect life! I had a beautiful home, an excellent checking and savings account, a vacation home, and I worked for one of the top private jet companies in the world. So, I got to travel the world expense-free. I have met some fascinating men, and most of them have been wealthy white men.

Don't get me wrong, I have had my share of sugar daddies, but I always got excited when there were handsome black men that flew on the Smithsonian Private Jet. I walked around the cabin, making sure everything was intact. I went to the liquor cabinet and pulled down four cognac glasses and a bottle of Dussé.

Mr. Harrison, the head pilot walked into the main cabin and said, "Our favorite passenger is about to board."

I nodded my head, getting into a professional stance. My eyes did all the smiling that my face couldn't. Maxwell Milan was boarding the cabin, and I couldn't have been happier. Mr. Milan had his hands in a few small business ventures, but his bread and butter were the dispensaries he owned in California, Colorado, D.C., and Hawaii.

He brought in millions of dollars every year, but it wasn't his socioeconomic status that excited me. He was gorgeous! He stood at 6'5", he had hazel eyes that complimented his smooth, dark chocolate skin, his full cocoa lips that were surrounded by a neatly trimmed goatee. His sexy hands were adorned with neatly manicured nails that I couldn't wait to suck on. What made him seem like the sexiest man alive was his confidence; he always stood with his back straight, and his shoulders held high, and I loved that.

He walked up to us and said, "I hope we have safe travels this afternoon Mr. Harrison."

Mr. Harrison smiled and said, "Definitely, Clear skies all the way to Mykonos."

I tried to hide my excitement. Mykonos has always been one of my dream vacations, and although I would just be passing through, I was still happy about it.

Maxwell smiled at me and took my hand in his and said, "It's nice to see you again, Ms. Washington."

"The pleasures all mine Mr. Milan," I said.

After all the formalities were over, we boarded the jet. I smiled as I showed him to his usual seat. There was something so intriguing about Maxwell, and it killed me that I couldn't put my finger on it. I know one thing's for sure, I knew he took a liking to me. There were a total of 10 female flight attendants, that worked for Smithsonian Airlines. And not one of them had ever flown with Maxwell.

Co-pilot Lowry came in and said, "Mr. Milan, we are preparing takeoff in the next 25-30 minutes."

"No rush guys, I want us to have safe travels, so take all the time you need," Maxwell said.

I rolled my eyes. I hated when we had to wait before takeoff. To kill time, I walked around, making sure everything was in its right place. I was trying to work off some nervous energy. Maxwell made my body quiver without even touching me, so I knew that my panties would melt off me, if I got close to him. I finally made my way over to him, asking if he needed anything.

"No, I'm fine, thank you," he said.

Another 15 minutes passed, and Mr. Harrison informed me that we're ready for takeoff. I stood in my designated position and began to give my safety speech. I told Mr. Milan that all his devices needed to go into airplane mode, but he could use the jet's Wi-Fi. I showed him how to use the oxygen mask and life jacket if needed. Lastly, I showed him the emergency exits.

"We have a 14 and half hour flight ahead of us, so there will be plenty of refreshments and food. Smithsonian Airlines is happy to be at your service as we grace the Friendly Skies," I said.

Maxwell smiled once I was finished, but his eyes were devouring me. I took my seat and fastened my seatbelt until we were cruising at a safe altitude.

Four hours into our flight...

We had been cruising for some time, and I would have enjoyed being at Mr. Milan's beck and call, but he didn't want shit. I was beginning to think he wasn't feeling me as much as I thought. I decided to test the waters; the sun was starting to set, so I began to close all the shades. Once I made it over to him, I exposed a little more cleavage, then leaned over him.

"Sorry, Mr. Milan, just closing the shades," I said.

"You're fine," he said.

I could hear him inhale my scent. I was even more surprised when he leaned into me and flicked his tongue across my neck. I just knew I had creamed my panties.

"Why are you playing with me?" he whispered.

I bit the inside of my cheek and whispered back, "Nobody's playing."

He sucked my earlobe into his mouth, then slid his fingers up my skirt. My moans hitched in my throat.

"Oh my god," I moaned.

His index and middle fingers were working their way inside of me as his thumb worked my clit. He kissed along my jawline and neck, and then he used his other hand to rub my nipples. My peircings made my nipples extremly sensitive. My right nipple was hanging over my tank top; he rolled it between his thumb and middle fingers. I felt like I was floating. So I could only imagine what his dick felt like.

He worked his fingers deeper in me and said, "Damn, I knew you would have some good pussy."

I bit my lip as I started to grind on his hand. Our moment was cut short. I began to panic when I heard one of the pilots messing with the entry door.

"I'm fucking you before we land in Greece. Now straighten yourself up," he whispered.

He quickly pulled his hand from my skirt and went back to looking over some documents. I stumbled back, pulling my skirt down and fixing my titties. I took a professional stance, just as Co-pilot Lowry was coming in.

"Are you guys okay back here?" he asked.

Before I could say anything, Maxwell said, "Yes, we're fine, thanks for checking."

I nodded my head in approval when Lowry looked at me. Once he went back to the pilot cabin, I quickly went to the overhead that held my luggage and pulled out my duffle bag. *Mr. Vibe* was lying flat on my laptop. I smiled and looked at Maxwell. He was enthralled in his work.

So, I snuck off to the bathroom and locked the door. I sat on top of the sink and propped my legs up. I slid my panties to the side and dipped my finger inside me to see how wet I was. My juices slid down my hand. I set *Mr. Vibe* on the right setting and put him on my clit. My eyes immediately rolled to the back of my head, thinking about how good his fingers felt inside me. I slowly moved the tip around on my engorged clitoris.

"Oh my god! That feels so good," I moaned.

I began to move my hips in a figure-eight motion and could feel my nectar sliding down my thigh. The rabbit continued flicking my pearl, while the shaft glided in and out of me. I bit my lip to keep from screaming. All I could think about was how good Maxwell would feel deep inside of me. My leg started shaking, and I knew I was about to cum everywhere, but I quickly caught myself. I wanted to cream all over Maxwell's chocolate pipe.

I slid down and set *Mr. Vibe* in the sink, running hot water over the toy. I took a wad of paper towel and wet it, then cleaned my legs off. Once I knew my mind was in the right place, I walked back into the main cabin. I bent down to put my toy back in my bag, then in the overhead. I looked back at Maxwell, and he gave me a sly grin. I bit my lip. This was going to be a long flight.

Eight hours later...

Maxwell and I had found ourselves; playing a game of cat and mouse. If I seemed like I wasn't paying him any attention, he would do something to make me look his way. If he appeared not to be paying me any mind, I would do something outlandish to get his attention. I was standing by the counter when I let my titties free. Allowing their natural perkiness to bounce and sway.

When he finally looked my way, he licked his lips and let his eyes devour me. I couldn't wait for him to suck my nipples like Hershey's kisses. I smiled at him as I lifted one of my titties and flicked my tongue across my hardened nipple. I could tell this was getting to him. When I knew I had him all riled up, I slowly put my breast back into my bra. He wiped his mouth as I smirked.

I turned away from him to act like I was working. I heard him stand up, and I turned around as he unbuckled his belt and unzipped his pants. He pulled his long, hard dick out and let it bounce up and down. My mouth watered, and I was tempted to get on my knees and suck it. He wrapped his big hand around his lengthy shaft and slowly stroked up & down.

My gaze stayed fixated on his movement; I tried to match his rhythm. He had his bottom lip pulled in as his eyes remained fixed on me. I squeezed my thighs tighter, as the tingling began to wash over me. I wanted so badly to be on my knees, encouraging him to get his nut, begging him to nut on my tongue, my face, my titties. I wanted to tell him how I couldn't wait to taste his babies.

Before I could walk over to him, he abruptly stopped and stuffed his still hard dick back into his slacks. I let out a frustrated breath. I was tired of this nigga playing. I wanted that dick now! He took his seat and asked me for a drink. I rolled my eyes, pulling down one of the cognac glasses. I put an ice cube in it, then poured a third of Dussé into his glass. I swirled it around for a minute letting the cognac mingle with the ice.

"Here you go, Mr. Milan," I said, walking over to him.

He wrapped his hand around mine when he grabbed his drink. My body heated up another 20 degrees. He took one of my fingers, dipped it in his glass, and then sucked my finger into his warm mouth. A moan hitched in my throat. This man had me so turned on that my clit started riding my thong. I snatched away from him and quickly walked to the back.

10 minutes later...

I returned from the restroom, and I watched as co-pilot Lowry walked over to Maxwell and then bent down. He nodded in approval as Maxwell seemed to be giving him some type of instruction.

"Sounds good, Mr. Milan," Lowry said.

Another five minutes had passed, and Lowry walked over to me and said, "Kourtnyí, you are officially off the clock. Enjoy your vacation."

I was a bit confused, but when I saw Maxwell staring at me, I knew he had something to do with this.

"Okay, great, thank you so much," I said, shaking his hand.

I waited until Lowry went back to the pilot cabin, then turned my back towards Maxwell. I didn't need to look at him to know he had gotten up. I could feel his energy. Once he got close enough to me, he pressed his hard-on into my ass. He pulled my braids to the side and kissed my neck.

"Mr. Milan, this is rea...lly unprofessional," I said as he kissed me.

"Baby, don't worry about that. They are not coming back here for the rest of the flight," he said.

He picked up the bottle of Dussé, taking four huge sips. I could feel his dick growing stiffer.

"I thought you weren't gonna stay true to your promise," I said.

I began helping him unbutton my jacket.

"I'm always a man of my word, baby. I was waiting for the right moment. As I said, you're getting fucked before we land."

Those words made my punany pucker with excitement. He tossed my jacket to the side and then pulled my tank top over my head. I turned around so I could finally see his face. I hungrily slid my tongue in his mouth. He unsnapped my bra and held my titties in his hand. He admired them and smiled at my nipple piercings. He bent down and slowly licked 'em from top to bottom.

"Ooohh shit," I moaned.

He grabbed a couple of ice cubes and rubbed them around my nipples. My body was on fire. I felt like I was floating on a cloud, and he hadn't even pulled his dick out yet. The way he touched me was soft and tender, yet firm. He licked my neck, sucked my chin, then pulled on my bottom lip. I tried to unbuckle his belt, but he pushed my hands away as we continued to kiss.

"I wanna taste you," he moaned into my mouth.

I laughed and asked, "Where am I going to get comfortable?"

He turned me around, so my back was pressed against his hard chest and stomach.

He wrapped his hand around my neck, and said, "You can worry about being comfortable in Mykonos. Right now, live in the moment."

He continued to suck and bite on my neck, and then he slid his fingers back down my skirt.

"Oh my god!" I moaned.

He toyed with my clit until I was ready to cum. When my nails dug into his skin. He pulled his fingers from between my legs and painted my lips with my cream. I hungrily sucked them and cleaned his fingers off. He unzipped my skirt and told me to get on top of the bar counter on all fours.

"Dayum, you look so good, Kourtnyí. You don't know how long I've been waiting to eat this pussy," He moaned.

I looked back at him and said, "Then come eat, daddy."

I didn't have to ask twice. He smiled, then smacked my ass. He used his big hands to spread my ass further apart before burying his face in it. My eyes rolled to the back of my head as he ate my pussy and ass. Maxwell's tongue had to be made of gold, the way it slithered between both holes. He was driving me crazy. He pulled my thong to the side and rubbed his thumb over my asshole before spitting on it and sliding his thumb in me.

"Ooohh shit, your tongue feels so good," I moaned.

"You like that shit, huh? I love eating this good shit, you gon' give me a cavity," he moaned.

His tongue slowly replaced his thumb. I bit down on my lip.

"Daddy, I'm ready for that dick," I said, grabbing the back of his neck.

He continued feasting on me like I was his plate at Thanksgiving. He didn't stop until I came all over his face.

I heard him unzip his pants, and he leaned into my ear and asked, "You sure you can take all this dick?"

I nipped his lip and said, "Nigga quit playing and put that dick in me."

We kissed. Our tongues doing a sensual tango.

"Turn around," he demanded.

I happily obliged. He stepped closer to me, and I helped guide him into my slippery hole. We both let out a gasp, his length, and girth stretching me out.

"Damn, girl, you feel better than I imagined," he groaned.

I smiled, glad that I had been consuming his thoughts. We stayed still for about five minutes. We were getting acquainted with the feel of each other.

"Now I'm about to beat this thang up," he said.

"C'mon and give it to me then," I taunted.

He sucked my earlobe into his mouth as he began to find his groove. Honey, when he did, I couldn't do anything but scream his name.

"Yes, fuck me! Oh my, that dick so big," I groaned.

He bit my chin and teased, "Tell me you love this dick because I love this pussy."

My eyes rolled to the back of my head as he continued to stroke my creamy walls. I wrapped my arms around his neck and dug my nails into his shoulder as he pounded my cunt.

"Oh yeah, I'm on that spot. Go ahead and cream on your dick, baby."

I dug my nails deeper into his skin, and in one swift motion, he had my legs in the crook of his arms. We were in the middle of the cabin fucking like it was nobody's business.

"Maxwell, daddy... you on my spot! Nigga yes!" I yelled.

"I love how you moan my name, baby. I ain't letting up on that spot until you cream all over my pipe," he said.

He continued to go harder and deeper. His balls smacking against my ass was music to my ears. I was so close to cumming, but he kept teasing me. He held my wrist in his hands to keep me from scratching him. One of the pilots came over the intercom, letting us know we were getting ready to experience high turbulence in the last 45 minutes of our flight. Baby did things get intense! Between the turbulence and Maxwell beating my walls down. I felt like I was having an out-of-body experience.

"Nigga I'm about to cum. Oh my, fuck daddy!" I groaned.

"There you go, baby. C'mon and cum on your dick. This pussy gon' have a nigga going crazy," he said.

As the turbulence shook the plane, Maxwell held onto me tighter. Just as the turbulence eased up, my walls started to contract, and I was cumming all over him.

"Whew, shit," I said as we kissed.

"Got damn girl! That was perfect," he said, placing kisses on my neck.

He still had my legs in the crook of his arms as I said, "Mr. Milan, you are a dangerous man."

He smirked and said, "I told you, I keep my promises."

I laughed as he let me down. My legs felt like overcooked noodles, but he helped me stand up. We shared another kiss when I noticed he still had a hard-on.

"You ready for round two?" he asked, smacking my ass.

I smiled and said, "Yeah, but this time I'm in control."

He walked back over to his seat, sat down, and said, "You got it, baby."

I climbed on top, riding him until we landed in Greece.

Nympho 9

College Hook-ups Pt. I

Collegе is stressful as fuck! You have back-to-back due dates for papers, quizzes that turn into 250-point test, and professors not understanding that you have a life outside of classes. You would be ready to tear your fucking hair out! But one way many of us relieved our stress was by fucking. When it came to releasing my frustrations, I kept all it bottled up. I wasn't too keen on fucking any ole body. The man I wanted, was oblivious to the fact I was on fire for his fine ass. Whenever I laid eyes on him, all I could think about was him blowing my back out.

There was a point where we could have been in a relationship. But it didn't work out that way. So, it was just me and my fantasies. I loved how his brown skin looked so hard yet soft at the same time. His thick Dominican accent always made me weak in the knees. I knew he had a bomb ass physique underneath his clothes, which came from years of playing football. Whenever you saw him, he always had a mean mug on his face, but once he was comfortable around you, he had a beautiful smile. The way he would look at me, always made my coochie come alive!

It had been a few months since we last spoke. I didn't want him to think I was reaching out, because the word on campus was he just got shitload of money, and he had just crossed into the hottest fraternity on campus. He was lowkey, to begin with, so I know all of this unwanted attention was making him uncomfortable.

So, every now and then, I would text Santiago to let him know if he ever wants to talk, I'm here. My efforts were going unnoticed, so I decided to let him be and just focus on finishing the semester strong. But my yearning for him never went away.

Three weeks later...

I was going through my room, packing and trashing all the unnecessary shit I bought throughout the semester. While I was cleaning out my closet, I realized I still had Tiago's canteen he let me use. A sly smile made its way across my face as I started to devise a plan. I rushed into my room and picked up my phone to text him.

Me: *Hey, I still have your canteen you let me use some time ago. When do you wanna come and get it?*

I waited patiently for a response.

Santiago: *Whenever you want me to come and get it, baby.*

I was taken aback by him calling me baby because, before that, he seemed to have no interest in me. But I decided to ignore it.

Me: *I'm free later today. But it's really up to you, just let me know when you're free.*

Santiago: *Bet.*

After that, I went on about my day, lowkey forgetting about our conversation.

Later that night...

I was chilling with my best friends, having a good ghetto time, when I got a text from Santiago.

Santiago: *Wya?*

I looked at my phone, puzzled because I didn't know why he would be asking me that.

"Y'all, why did Santiago just ask me where I'm at," I said.

I wasn't expecting them to answer.

"Girl, that's because he about to give you some dick," one of my best friends Jamal said.

I laughed and texted him back.

Me: *Heading to my room, what's up?*

I listened to Jamal, Malcolm, my other best friend, and Derek (Jamal's boyfriend) continue with their conversation.

Santiago: *I'm heading to campus to get my canteen.*

Me: *Okay, cool, I'm heading to my room now.*

Santiago: *Bet, I'm leaving my house now. Be there in 20.*

Me: *Okay, cool.*

I got up, grabbed my bookbag, and headed toward the door.

"What's going on?" Malcolm asked.

"He's coming to pick up his canteen," I answered.

"Nah, he coming to pick up that pussy," Derek said.

I laughed and walked out of the room.

But before the door could close, I walked back in and said, "But this doesn't make any sense."

"Girl, it doesn't matter, hurry up and get to your room and shower," Jamal said.

"Alright." With that, I finally left Jamal's room and hauled ass back to my dorm.

30 minutes later...

I had just gotten out of the shower when Santiago texted saying he was about 10 minutes away and asked if I could meet him in the lobby. I let out a sigh because this man didn't know how bad I wanted him in my guts.

While I was putting coconut oil on my body, I was trying to devise a plan. I looked over at my wall and smiled at my keys. I took them from their hanging place and put them in my bag.

Hoping my plan would work. Right on time, as I suspected, my phone was ringing.

"Hello," I answered.

"Yeah, you can come to the lobby," he said.

"Actually, could you come up to my room. I misplaced my keys, and I don't want to be locked out," I said.

"That's fine. What's your room number?" he asked. "505," I said.

"Okay, 505, I'm on my way up," he said.

I hung up the phone. I waited for about two minutes, and he walked through the door.

"Karis," he sang in his accent.

"I'm right here," I said, peaking my head out of my room.

I handed him the canteen as he walked into my space.

"Thank you so much," he said.

"No problem."

I watched him take a seat on the corner of my desk while we stared at each other.

"How have you been?" I asked.

He shook his head and said, "I've been cool, how about you. You good?" He asked.

I shrugged my shoulders and told him I had seen better days. A shiver went down my spine as he licked his lips and stared me up and down. His voice dropped an octave, and he toyed with the charm on my necklace.

"What's that on your neck?" He asked.

"It's an Ankh," I said.

"I know what it is, but do you know what it means?"

"Yeah, it's the Egyptian cross; it represents life and fertility," I stated.

He gave me a sly smile and said, "I see you got a little knowledge."

We laughed as I nudged him and said, "Boy, don't try and play me like that."

We spent the next few minutes catching up.

"You got a man in your life?" He asked.

"Nope, you know I don't fool with these clowns up here. But I know you must have a lucky lady," I teased.

He shook his head and folded his arms across his chest.

"People have been acting funny towards me ever since I got all that money and crossed. Girls, I ain't never seen before coming up to me and trying to give me some play..." --he paused--

"My brothers been expecting me to clean their shit up and asking for money left and right. You know I ain't with all that," he vented.

I rubbed his shoulders and told him I'm always here if he needs someone to vent too.

"Yeah, I just need a break from everything, but let me go see what these niggas want," he said, getting up.

He got up and stretched; his scent overtook my room.

"C'mon bring it in," he said.

I stepped into him, and he wrapped me tight in his strong arms. I could feel myself melting in his embrace.

"I'll see you later," he said, looking at me. Before I knew what came over me.

I kissed him.

To be continued.

Nympho 10

My 2 Lovers

I like to believe that I am a woman who is in control of my sexuality. Which in translation means I love to fuck! I loved having my back blown out and having a long, thick pipe hitting against my spot. It's the reason why I'm dating two men right now; it's nothing serious with either of them. They both have different qualities that attract me to them. They both give me mind-blowing sex, and lately, I've had the desire for both of them to be inside of me. Isaac was tall and had a slim build. He had a wild, untamed afro with a neatly trimmed goatee that perfectly surrounded his juicy red lips.

He had a great sense of humor and was a struggling artist. Whenever I was with Isaac, I was bound to have a great time, and the lining eaten out of my pussy. Now Horus, on the other hand, was beautiful and stimulated me on a level beyond sex. Horus's parents were from Egypt, so he had an exotic look to him. He had smooth dark skin with light brown eyes. He was on the shorter side and had a stocky build.

He always wore his beautiful, locs pulled back, so they hung in the middle of his shoulder blades. He also worked as a mechanic and had a rugged look to him. The one thing I loved most about Horus was his intellect. We always had something to talk about, and I learned something new whenever we hung out.

The sex was amazing, always filled with passion, and I loved it when he called me his chocolate beauty. Most importantly, Isaac and Horus were both freaky ass men, willing to try any and everything. I was getting wet just thinking about it. This weekend, I had something special planned for them both.

Two nights later...

I was on FaceTime with Isaac, and he looked damn good.

"How's the piece coming along?" I asked sipping my wine.

He looked straight into the camera with his dark dreamy eyes.

"It's coming. You look so good. Mmmpph, I can't wait to fuck them chocolate titties," he said.

I blushed and said, "You are making me, so wet right now. I miss you."

"Oh yeah," he said seductively.

I sat my glass of wine down on the nightstand. And I shimmied out of my nightgown. I grabbed both of my breasts and flicked my tongue around my dark nipples. Isaac looked on in amazement as he groped himself over the thick fabric of his paint-covered jeans.

"Dayum, I can't wait to paint you," he said.

I smiled and said, "Unzip your pants and stroke yourself."

I slid my fingers between my slick folds and had my first

mini orgasm. I didn't want Isaac to cum yet. I wanted him to save all that thick, gooey nut for this weekend. I bought my fingers up to my lips and licked my juices off.

"Damn Bianca, you are such a tease," he laughed, stuffing his hard-on back in his jeans.

"I have something really special planned for us this weekend," I said.

"Baby, my schedule is already cleared"

"Okay, I'll see you Saturday at 7," I said, hanging up.

Two days later, I texted Horus to clear his schedule for the weekend and be at my place, Saturday at 7. He texted back, telling me he couldn't wait to see me. A sly smile spread over my full lips as I became excited for this weekend.

Saturday Evening...

I was standing in my vanity, giving myself the once over. I had on a pair of chocolate brown, Red bottoms, a red lace lingerie set; my dark-skinned shimmered under the lighting, and my long hair was curled to perfection.

Then I did the once over of my condo. Rose petals decorated the living room, hallway, and bedroom. All of the lights were dimly lit; I had a bowl of strawberries and honey and two bottles of champagne on ice. I wasn't the most creative person I knew, but I must admit that I outdid myself. I lit a couple of candles and took a sip of my drink. As I was about to pour another one, there was a knock at my door.

I opened my robe just enough to show off my ample cleavage. I went to open the door, and Isaac looked delicious in his all black. He had his 'fro braided neatly to the back. He was slack-jawed, looking at me. He walked in and shut the door.

"Fuck! Baby, you look sexy, turn around, let me see you," he said.

I gave him a quick spin as he slapped my ass.

"That's a lot of wagon you draggin' boo," he said, pulling me into him.

I started laughing as his tongue explored my mouth. I didn't want things to get freaky just yet; unbeknownst to Isaac, we were still waiting on Horus's slow ass. Isaac started sucking my nipples through my lace, and the crotch of my panties dampened. We heard a knock at my door.

"Are you expecting someone else?" Isaac asked.

I ignored him and raced to the door. Horus walked in, in a pair of black dickies, Timbs, and a long sleeve shirt that hugged his muscles just right.

"How are you, my chocolate beauty?" Horus asked, kissing me.

"Yo! Bianca, who the fuck is this!" Isaac yelled.

"Yeah, Bianca, who is this?" Horus co-signed.

I saw my evening slowly crumbling before my eyes, so I quickly explained that I had been dating them for the past six and a half months.

"I've wanted both of you at the same time," I said, bringing them close to me; they both smacked their lips.

"Y'all would do anything for me, right?" I asked, looking at them.

I could feel their bulges thickening, and I knew common sense was about to fly out the window. I unbuckled and unzipped their pants and started playing with their ever-growing pipes. I got down on my knees and put both of them in my mouth. Groans escaped from their mouths, as I took turns sucking their dicks.

"Bianca, you want tonight to be all about you, right?" Horus asked.

I nodded my head in a yes manner while putting both of their engorged heads in my wet mouth.

He pulled me up and said, "Then it's your night, baby."

I was in pure ecstasy as I laid on my back. Wet lips and tongues created cool streaks on my heated skin. Thick, long fingers fucked into my pussy and ass. They both took turns sucking on my nipples, and Isaac was the first to go down and feast on me. He flattened his tongue against my swollen pearl, and a gasp escaped my lips. Horus leaned down and slithered his tongue between my lips.

"She tastes good, doesn't she?" Horus asked, playing with my nipples.

"Hell yeah," Isaac said, dipping his tongue into my cream-filled hole.

"Oh my god!" I screamed.

Isaac and Horus traded places, and Isaac fed me his tongue. I loved the taste of my essence being fed to me.

"Y'all are driving me crazy," I moaned.

Horus lifted up, licked his cum slick lips, and beat his dick against my pussy. Isaac held my legs up, and Horus slid into me.

"This pussy so good and juicy," Horus moaned.

Isaac licked his fingers and made a circular pattern around my clit. They took turns fucking into my pussy and ass and creaming my cunt. When Isaac finally pulled out, they flipped me over like I was a rag doll.

"You wanted us both inside you, right?" Isaac asked.

I nodded my head, yes.

"That's what you about to get."

Isaac laid on his back, I climbed on top of him, and Horus was in the back of me. Horus held my ass open and spit in between my cheeks. Issac slid in first, then Horus's meaty pipe was sliding in next. Words couldn't explain the bliss my pussy, ass, and I were feeling. My eyes rolled to the back of my head as incoherent sounds came from my throat.

"Yeah, baby, arch that back so I can go deeper," Horus moaned.

"Fuck!" I yelled.

"Dayum, this feels so good," Isaac growled.

I bit into the pillow as they both tried to outstroke each other.

They took turns taunting one another:

"You like this dick?"

"Nah, she loves this dick."

"Tell this nigga this my pussy."

"Tell 'em, baby, this always been my pussy."

Horus smacked my ass like he was playing a set of bongos.

"Ooohh, Shit! Y'all fucking me so good!" I moaned.

My pussy muscles began to contract violently around their dicks. They were stretching me out in a delicious burn. Their love sticks started to thump inside of me. I knew they were getting ready to come. I swear I could see fireworks as all of us came together, and they released their heavy loads inside of me.

They both pulled out and watched as I pushed their nuts out. Isaac kissed me as Horus went down on me. After tonight's escapade, this needed to happen on a regular basis!

Nympho 11

The New Exec Pt. I

I was sitting in my office, with my skirt around my waist. I had my legs splayed open as I slid the long, black plastic dick in and out of my wet slit. I was fantasizing about one of the new executives that just got hired. He was some type of fine. He had this luscious brown skin, thick lips that I couldn't wait to suck my juices off, these large hands that would hold my breast as I rode him.

I pumped the dick in me faster as I felt my juices slide down my thighs. My eyes rolled to the back of my head as my walls tightened. As soon as I was about to cum; the new exec Tony walked into my office.

"I'm sorry, Miss Baker," he said.

He stood in the middle of my office shocked, not sure if he should leave or stay. So, I made the decision for him.

I was still playing with my pussy when I said, "No. Stay. Come join the party."

I didn't have to ask twice. He locked the door and slowly approached my desk. He lifted my leg and knelt between them. My kitty kat was staring him in the face.

"Damn, it smells delicious." He said.

I watched as he took the dildo out of my hand, and slowly fucked me with it, while eating my pussy. I put my hand on the back of his head to push his face deeper in my crotch. He shocked the shit out of me; when he pulled the dildo out of me and sucked my cream off. I was too turned on, to say anything. He placed the plastic dick to my lips, and I licked the rest of my juices off and licked around the head. I watched as Tony got up and unbuckled his slacks. I quickly got on my knees and sucked his enormous dick through his boxers.

"Dayum Shantél, that feels good," Tony moaned.

I smirked because I knew my head game was out of this world. And surprisingly his dick tasted amazing.

"Oh yeah, keep sucking that dick, girl," he said fucking my face.

I decided I wanted to get nasty with it; spit was flying everywhere, and I super soaked his heavy nuts. He announced he was getting ready to nut. I pulled his dick from my mouth and got up off my knees. I held his dick in my hand as we shared a wet, sloppy, tongue probing kiss. I pushed him in my chair, then climbed on my desk. My ass was high in the air, and the scent of my wet pussy invaded my office.

"Fuck, girl, you got a pretty ass and pussy," Tony said, playing with his dick.

I slowly slid my fingers in and out of my cunt. When I was ready for Tony, I looked back at him and moaned, "Come and get it, baby."

Tony got behind me, placed his hand on the arch of my back, then slid his dick into the back of my pussy. We both gasped in unison as his big dick stretched me out in a delicious burn.

"Damn, I didn't know you were so tight, baby," Tony growled, grinding into my ass.

"I know, baby, just keep going slow until all of you is in me," I moaned.

About five minutes later, Tony had all that big dick inside of me. He was knocking the bottom out of my pussy. Cunt juice splattered all over my desk.

"You like this pussy, Tony?"

"Hell yeah! My pipe's swimming in this wet shit," he groaned.

He pulled me by my hair and leaned over to kiss me. Tony started to power fuck me; he wrapped his hands around my neck, and his pelvis smacked into my ass.

"Smack it, daddy!" I yelled.

He slapped my ass like he was playing a set of bongos. The harder he smacked it, the more my cunt creamed.

"C'mon girl, work for this nut. Ride this dick from the back," Tony demanded.

I obliged his command. I rode that dick for dear life. I could tell I had him going through it when I started making it clap.

"Fuck, Shantél, I'm about to nut. Where you want it, baby?"

"I want it in my pussy! Fuck nut deep in my pussy!" I yelled.

Tony gripped my waist tight and pumped into me. I felt his dick thump inside me as my pussy tightened around him. A few seconds later, he was filling me with a hot, gooey nut. Tony pulled out of me and rubbed his nut all on my ass and asshole. He slipped his pipe in my ass. I almost fell over my desk; this nigga was dickin' me so good. My eyes crossed as my pussy walls contracted and cream dripped on my desk.

"Tony, that dick is so good," I moaned.

"Miss Baker, you're wanted in a conference in 15 minutes," my boss said.

"Dayum, that was a good fuck," Tony said smacking my ass.

"I know maybe we could do it again."

He nodded his head and put his clothes back on. I watched as he walked out of my office. I sat back in my chair and looked down at all the soaked papers lying on my desk. I relaxed as the smell of a freshly fucked cunt spread through my office. I felt at ease after bustin' that nut.

Nympho 12

College Hookups Pt. II

We gently pulled away from each other, and I said, "I'm sorry, I didn't mean to do all that."

"You cool chica, why did you stop?" He asked.

I started rambling on about how I thought he wasn't interested in me and how I let my WHOREmones get the best of me. He grabbed my face and kissed me again. Our tongues danced with one another.

He pulled on my bottom lip and said, "I've wanted you for so long."

Those words were like music to my ears. I smiled at him as my panties grew wetter.

"Don't you have to go talk to your brothers?" I asked as he kissed my neck.

"Fuck them, niggas," he said.

With that, we were kissing again. He pulled my tank top over my hand and held my titties in his strong hands. He licked and sucked on my nipples. Then he gently bit and rolled them between his thumb and forefinger.

Moans escaped my lips as he continued to caress my sensitive nipples. He kissed me again and sucked on my tongue. He picked me up and laid me on the bed. He worked on my titties some more and made a wet trail down my navel to my pussy. Santiago pulled my shorts off and spread my legs eagle. A sexy grin was on plastered on his face, as his sticky treat greeted him.

"Karis, baby, I've waited so long for this," he said, kissing my inner thigh.

"I have too, baby," I moaned.

I heard him inhale my sweet scent. He placed a kiss on my moist lips. As his thick, wet tongue traced my frame. My eyes rolled to the back of my head as he French kissed my nana. He gently spread my lips apart until my pink center greeted him.

"Tú coño es muy bonito chica," he whispered into my crotch.

Santiago flattened his tongue against my swollen pearl and sucked on it like it was a jeweled oyster. My breath hitched in my throat, and I ran my fingers through his curly hair. He grabbed both my wrist and held them in one hand. **My eyes rolled to the back of my head, and I managed to pull one of my hands from his grip and push his head away. His tongue game was out of this world, and he was causing multiple orgasms to shoot through my body.**

"Quit running, chica," he whispered into me.

I lost my mind when Santiago firmly but gently flicked his tongue on my swollen clit. He looked up at me with a smile in his eyes, and he finally came up for air, his face soaked with my juices. I sat up and saw the material of his jeans were constricting his hard-on. I pulled him closer to me, and hungrily kissed him. I loved how I tasted on his lips and tongue.

I rubbed his dick through his jeans, and I was pleasantly surprised with what he was packing. I pulled his shirt off, and my fingers ran down the crease in his chiseled chest. I unzipped his jeans, and his pipe sprung out before I had a chance to greet it. I smiled and rubbed his precum over the head.

"I want you to beat my pussy up, papí," I whispered, sucking on his earlobe. He wore a mischievous smile.

"Lay back, and let me take care of you, Mamí," he said.

I did as I was told and played in my sticky honey pot as I watched him stroke his long pipe. We both had a hunger in our eyes; we wanted to devour each other.

He continued stroking himself and asked, "Do you have any condoms?"

Still playing in my wetness, I pointed to where they were on my desk. We shared a knowing laugh. I watched as he rolled a Magnum down his thick shaft. He pulled me by my ankle to the edge of the bed and tasted me again. I pushed his face further into my crotch until I couldn't take it anymore.

"Boy, quit playing and put that dick in me!" I yelled.

He finally climbed on the bed and threw my legs over his strong shoulders. He worked the tip in; I gasped as I felt him stretch my walls.

"C'mon chica; I got you. I'm not gone hurt you, baby," he whispered.

He wined his hips until all of him was inside me.

"Oh, my Gawd! This dick so big!" I yelled.

His eyes rolled to the back of his head. He pulled his bottom lip in, and he kept telling me how wet and tight my coño is. He leaned down to suck on my titties and kiss me. When we found our groove, it was on and popping. He kissed and sucked on my neck and tatas.

He licked my ear and whispered, "Chica me encanta este coño. Es tan húmedo y apretado."

I don't know what the hell he just said, but I know it made me tighten my walls around him.

"Oh my.... fuck.... you are fucking me so good papí," I moaned.

He smoothed my hair down and said, "Sí mamí."

I leaned up to kiss him. I hungrily sucked on his tongue and lips. He started to stroke faster. I closed my eyes tight because he was hitting my spot.

Santiago wrapped his hand around my neck and said, "Open them pretty eyes and look at me while I'm fucking my pussy."

I loved it when a man was dominate during sex. It made me cream harder. I tried my best to keep my eyes open. I nearly lost my mind when he brought my feet up to his face and sucked on my toes.

"This my pussy now, chica."

"Yes, yes, yes, it's your pussy. It's always been your pussy papí!" I screamed.

I could feel my walls tighten around him as he kept pumping in and out of me.

"Yeah, this coño so wet and creamy chica," he moaned.

He started groaning in my ear. He put my legs in the crook of his arms, then all of a sudden, he was lifting me up in the air.

He was gliding in and out of me while we were standing on the twin mattress. The only sounds that could be heard through my room were the faint sounds of the tv, my wet pussy being beat-up, and our moans & groans. I'm sure my roommate was getting an earful!

"Yes, nigga, yes! Fuck this pussy, beat this phat pussy up, boy," I moaned. He pushed my back against the wall and continued to beat my walls for dear life.

"Yeah, chica. Baby, you feel so good, you're huggin' me so right. I wanna bust bad," he said in my ear.

I pulled him closer to me so we could kiss. I couldn't get over how good his dick felt. Now, I was right at the edge, and my walls became tighter. I dug my nails into his back.

"Oh, my Gawd! Santiago baby, I'm about to cum!"

He laid me down on my back again and started playing with my engorged clit.

"Oh shit, fuck, yes! Fuck me, daddy. Fuck this pussy!"

He got into a push-up position, and his strokes became faster and more rigid. I felt his dick thump inside me.

"Karis, chica cum with me, baby!" He yelled.

I dug my nails deeper into his back as he sucked on my neck and titties.

"Fuck, chica! Yes papí! Shit, damn fuck!"

We screamed in unison as we came hard, holding onto each other. He leaned down and fed me his tongue as we kissed. I pushed him out of me, and I helped him pull the rubber off and flicked it across my room.

I kissed him again and asked, "Are you going to see your

brothers?"

He laughed and said, "Nah, them niggas can figure their own shit out. I'm with my baby," he said.

I was smiling so hard that I thought my face might get stuck. I couldn't believe he was all mine. He pulled me closer into him and kissed my forehead as he wrapped his arms around me.

"Next time, we're going to my place so I can wax that ass all over," he said.

I smiled again, mentally checking this off of my goal list for the semester.

Nympho 13

Couple's Retreat Pt. I

It had been almost eight years since my wife, and I had seen our best friends Keni and Tyree. It was a welcomed surprise when Tyree called and asked if Selena and I would like to go on a couple's vacation. We both said hell yeah. Shit, we needed a break from our hectic lives, and this was the perfect getaway. I smiled as I watched my wife come from the closet with a handful of clothes.

"I see somebody is excited?" I teased.

She laughed, "Shut up, Marcus."

I laughed too and asked, "Have you and Keni been talking?"

"Oh my god, yes, catching up on all the things. I can't lie. I missed my girl," she said.

"I know right. Shit, I've missed my boy, so hopefully, this trip brings back a lot of memories from college," I said.

"We had no business being that wild," Selena chuckled.

I smacked her ass agreeing with her. We started reminiscing about our days at TSU, and memories came flooding back. The room grew quiet, and I knew what was on both of our minds.

"When you and Tyree, have spoken has he mentioned their open marriage?" Selena asked.

"Nah, it hasn't come up," I answered.

I rubbed my goatee, deep in thought, unbeknownst to Selena, that was the biggest reason why I wanted us to stop hanging out with them. I didn't want them getting the wrong idea about us. Years ago, I made up this story to Selena, telling her that Tyree and I got into this big ass argument, and I wasn't fucking with him no more.

"Have you and Keni talked about it?" I asked.

She started smiling and said, "We have."

I didn't like that she seemed interested in that.

"You been getting any ideas?" I asked, not trying to hide my attitude.

Selena chuckled, "Boy, stop being so damn sensitive. No, I'm not getting any ideas."

She stepped towards me and whispered in my ear, "Your dick is the only one I want inside of me."

My attitude softened as she kissed my neck and collarbone. Then she made a wet trail down my abs and pulled my pipe from my boxers. It bounced up and down. My knees buckled as she swallowed me whole. If this trip allowed my wife to unleash her inner freak, I was more than happy to go on this couple's retreat.

Friday Evening: Couple's Retreat, The Smokey Mountain Cabins...

I grabbed our luggage out of the car as she excitedly watched three couples walk into the massive cabin.

"You think they're still coming?" Selena asked.

"Girl calm down. Tyree just texted me and said they're on the next shuttle," I explained.

Another two minutes went by, and the last shuttle pulled up. Tyree and Keni were the last ones to get off the bus. Selena and Keni both ran to each other and hugged.

"Oh, my God! Girl, you look good," they said to each other.

Tyree and I shared a brotherly embrace and watched with excitement as our wives continued to compliment each other. Although it was dark outside, I could tell Keni looked terrific. She had picked up weight in all the right places, and she had her dark hair cut low. I couldn't lie; the girl was still fine.

"Don't act like we ain't standing here," Tyree said.

"Boy shut up," Keni said, walking over to me.

I watched as my wife hugged Tyree, and they lingered a lil' too long for my liking.

Keni sensing my energy whispered, "Stop acting like that."

I rolled my eyes and pulled away from her. Selena and Tyree finally pulled away from each other. Out of the four of us, Selena and Tyree knew each other the longest.

"Man, we look damn good! I can't believe it's been almost ten years since we last saw each other," Tyree explained.

We shook our heads in approval. "I know right, I've missed y'all. I see that beard finally connecting Ree," Selena joked.

We all were cracking up.

"Yeah, okay, I see you still got jokes. I wish I could take all the praise for this luxurious beard, but my wife had a lot to do with it," Tyree explained winking.

Keni walked back to her husband, and they kissed. I looked over at Selena, who had a big smile on her face.

"Aiight y'all, what we about to get into?" I asked.

"Well, me and my homegirl are about to go into this nice ass cabin, chill on the lower balcony, and open a bottle of wine," Keni said.

"That sounds good to me," Selena agreed.

Me and Tyree both laughed as we watched the ladies hug again and laugh, walking up the steps.

"C'mon dawg, as soon we get this luggage in, we can come back out here and have a blunt," Tyree said.

I nodded my head, letting him know that I was down. I laughed to myself, hoping this week wouldn't be a regret.

Three days later...

I had a towel wrapped around me as I walked back to the bedroom. I may have spoken too soon. The trip itself has been incredible, but me and my wife were another story.

"Selena, what's wrong?" I asked.

She had been slamming and throwing stuff around all

morning. So, I knew she had an attitude.

"Nothing," she said.

I rolled my eyes and asked again, "Are you sure?"

She stood in place for a second, then asked, "Why haven't you and Tyree been hanging out?"

I shrugged my shoulders, not sure how to answer.

"We've grown apart. We're not the same anymore," I explained.

"So, you're still tripping about something that happened over eight years ago?" she asked sarcastically.

I stretched out on top of the bed and replied, "No, I'm not."

She chuckled.

"Whatever you say, but you've been an ass this entire trip, and I don't know why..."—she paused— "But if you and Tyree's falling out had anything to do with them having an open marriage, you need to grow up and be more open-minded," she said.

Now I was getting pissed.

I bit my lip and said, "As I said, we ain't fall out because of that."

"Whatever, but honestly, Marcus, you need to stop being so uptight. You have been an asshole this entire trip," she pouted.

She was right. I could have stayed home for all this bullshit. I was hoping we'd come on this trip and get our sex life back on track. But no, Keni was taking up all of her time.

I watched as she rolled her eyes and said, "Look, I'm not trying to argue with you, Marcus. Now let's forget about what I asked and enjoy the rest of this time with our friends and enjoy this couple's hike."

She started kissing me and playing with my dick. I hated that I was about to ruin this moment.

"Selena, that feels good, baby, but I'm not going on the hike," I said.

She stopped licking my head and punched me in this chest.

"Why not?" she asked angrily.

"Because the game is coming on," I said.

She nodded her head and said, "You know what? That's fine, Marcus."

I wiped my hand across my face. I watched as she grabbed her clothes and stormed off into the bathroom. Fuck! I knew I should've told Tyree's ass, we weren't coming on this trip. I decided I would let Selena calm down before we finished our discussion. I don't know what the fuck was going on with me. I was tired of being made out as the bad guy because I didn't want their lifestyle to influence Selena. I thought back to a conversation Selena and I were having the other night.

Saturday night...

We were lying up watching old episodes of Martin. Decades later and the shit is just as funny as it was when I first saw it. I looked over at my wife, and she was staring at me.

"What's up, boo?" I asked.

"How have you and Tyree been getting along?" she asked.

"I mean, it's been cool," I answered.

She nodded her head and asked, "Mmkay. Have y'all talked about their open marriage?"

I hid my smile, we talked about it in numerous conversations, but I wanted to play it cool.

"It's come up, but it ain't nothing we dwell on," I explained.

"Babe, you're good. I just wanted to know, that's all," she said.

I kissed her forehead. I was still on edge because I wasn't quite sure why she kept asking me about it. All of a sudden, she excitedly jumped up and hopped on top of me.

"Okay, okay! Since y'all have talked about it, I'm sure Tyree told you," she said.

I was lost, and confusion was written all on my face.

"Told me what?" I asked.

"That he's bi-sexual," she said.

Now I was thrown for a loop. This nigga really has changed.

"No, he didn't," I said, confusion laced my tone.

"Marcus don't act like that. If I made you uncomfortable, I'm sorry," she said, getting off me.

"You didn't make me uncomfortable. This shit's crazy, that's all," I said.

Selena shrugged her shoulders and admitted, "I don't think so."

I looked at my wife like she was crazy and questioned, "Since when you been into shit like that?"

"I always have, and you would know that if we had a conversa-

tion regularly, and if you weren't so closed-minded," she replied.

I ignored the close-minded comment.

"So, what? Are you gon' start doing gay shit to me now? Try and turn me out," I laughed.

"You are such an asshole! Nobody wants to turn you out. I find it sexy that a man can explore his sexuality, be confident and stand in it, is all I'm saying," she explained.

"Yeah, okay," I said, turning off the tv and the light.

I turned my back towards her, and she snatched all the cover off me.

Present...

Ever since Selena told me that shit about Tyree, I had been stirring clear of him. At the same time, I had so many questions. I shook the racing thoughts from my mind.

"Marcus, you tripping dawg," I said to myself.

I went and grabbed a beer, turned the game on, and I kicked my feet up, and began to relax.

∞∞∞

Later that evening...

"Well, when we get home, we can get our lawyers!" I yelled, slamming the door as I walked out of the bedroom.

I took the steps two at a time and stormed into the kitchen. I opened the fridge to grab a bottle of water and a plum. Then I took a seat on the countertop. This trip had to be the worst thing for my marriage. Instead of bringing us closer, it was tearing us apart. I was so lost in thought that I didn't hear somebody walk into the kitchen. I looked over my shoulder and saw Keni. She rolled her eyes at me and tried to leave the kitchen.

I grabbed her arm and asked, "Wait, Keni, can we talk?"

She made a hand gesture signaling me to start talking.

"What's going on with your girl? She has been tripping ever since we got here," I said.

Keni laughed and said, "I think you're confused. You're the one that's been tripping."

I shook my head and waved her off.

"Look, all I'm saying is you ain't hung out with none of us. From what I can see, you ain't been the best husband either," she explained.

"I work a lot, and I've been tired."

"That is no excuse. You wanna know something, Marcus?" she asked.

I shrugged my shoulders, not caring if she told me or not.

"I think you're jealous," she said in a sultry whisper.

"Ain't nobody jealous," I gritted.

"It's alright, you should live a little."

She stepped into me, pressing her body against mine. My dick was getting hard, and I couldn't deny that I've always wanted Keni.

"I've always wanted you," I whispered.

She smirked and said, "If I wanted you, I could have had you."

I licked my lips.

"Oh yeah," I said.

The sexual tension between us was thick. I wasn't sure who was going to make the first move.

"It's good to know that my husband isn't the only one wanting somebody's wife," Keni stated.

"What do you mean?" I asked.

"Tyree has always had a thing for Selena," she answered.

It threw me off a bit that she didn't seem upset about it.

"Man, please, that ain't gone happen. My wife ain't that type of woman," I shot back.

She started laughing. I was getting pissed because I wanted to know what was so damn funny.

"There's a lot about your wife you don't know," she smirked.

My blood was boiling because I didn't know if she was serious.

"Marcus, you need to calm down and stop being so damn scared and uptight," Keni said.

"I'm tired of y'all telling me that," I said, trying to walk away.

Keni grabbed my arm and said, "Relax."

Her hand traveled to my hard-on as she leaned up to kiss me. Then she kissed my neck and pulled my shorts underneath my ass.

"Ooohh, this dick is pretty," she moaned.

"Yeah, and he tastes better than he looks," I said.

I watched as she excitedly got on her knees and kissed the head. Pre-cum dripped down my thigh. I looked on in amazement as she lifted my dick and sucked on my balls. She licked the underside of my shaft and slowly put my pipe in her wet mouth. She throated me with ease, and she used her free hand to toy with my balls.

I palmed the back of her head so that I could fuck her throat. I grabbed her by the neck and slammed my dick across her full lips.

"Damn Keni," I moaned.

I leaned down so I could kiss her again.

I came back up, held my dick at the base, and started stroking her throat.

"There you go, baby. Let me get that neck," I moaned.

She pushed me back into the lower cabinets and sucked me up like a Hoover vacuum. She had my eyes rolling to the back of my head when she licked my gooch. I slightly bent my knees, so I could lean down and play with her nipples. I gently rolled them between my fingers. I tensed up when her tongue grazed my asshole.

"You were right; you do taste amazing," she moaned.

Keni was sucking my dick so sloppily that spit soaked the front of my shorts. I felt my toes curl in my sandals and my balls tighten. I knew I was about to nut.

"Damn, girl, I'm about to cum," I whispered.

My nut gushed out of me like a clogged facet finally being

cleaned. I was in awe; she didn't let one drop go to waste. She stood up, wiping the corners of her mouth. I couldn't help myself; I leaned down sucked on her light brown nipples. My dick was still hard.

"Let's find somewhere a lil' more private," I said.

"No, I gotta meet Tyree downstairs," she said.

I watched as she walked away, leaving my dick bouncing up and down. Damn! I wanted to fuck her on this countertop.

To be continued.

Nympho 14

Christmas Party

It was that time of year again, where people partied until the New Year, and common sense for most people seemed like a foreign concept. The company had thrown their yearly Christmas party, and for the most part, it was cool to see my colleagues cut loose and get drunk as hell. These were some uptight assholes, myself included, that took work way to serious.

I was hoping that one person would be here tonight, and that was my work wife, Naomi. We were always flirting with each other, and over the last few weeks, our sexual tension was building. Although I was here with my fiancé, I hoped Naomi didn't show up with anybody. I kept looking over at the entrance. So, I could spot her when she got here. Snapping me out of my thoughts was Mr. Cooper, the advertising executive.

"How are you doing tonight, Calvin?" He asked.

"I'm doing well, just enjoying everybody," I said.

"I see that you're not tossing them back like everybody else. Fiancé has you on a tight leash?" he asked.

I laughed and said, "Not at all; it's still early."

"Well, make sure you toss a few back. It makes it easier not to remember what you're going to regret in the morning," he said, walking away.

I laughed to myself.

"What's so funny?" my fiancé Candance asked.

"Nothing, one of my bosses, was talking to me," I said.

"Well, this is boring, and I wanna go home," she said.

I rolled my eyes and said, "Come on, it's still early, we leave now, we miss the crazy shit later."

She smacked her lips and said, "I guess. I'm giving it another hour, and if this party ain't picked up, I want to leave."

I cursed under my breath; she was throwing a monkey wrench in my plans.

"Alright, and then I'll make it up to you later," I said, kissing her cheek.

She smiled and said, okay. It was just my luck that Naomi walked into the ballroom. I watched as one of the waiters took her coat, and I couldn't help but lick my lips. She had on a red dress that stopped a few inches above her knees, and it complimented her dark-skin well, and she topped the outfit off with a pair of sexy ass nude Red Bottoms.

My smile disappeared when I noticed the stocky light-skinned brotha on her arm. Damn, now I needed to re-think my whole plan. I just might let Candance go home, I thought to myself. I decided I would let her greet everybody before approaching her, but I eyed her like a hawk.

I watched as she talked to a few executives and her assistant. It was finally my time to approach her, Candance had gone to the bathroom, and it seemed that Naomi's date was doing his own mingling. I put a little pep in my step and walked across the room to Naomi. I stood behind her but left some space between us so people wouldn't get the wrong idea.

"I didn't know you liked'em that light," I said.

She turned around and smiled.

"I can always count on you to joke about everything," she said.
"Who is he?" I asked.

She flashed that gorgeous smile and said, "Just a little arm candy for the night."

I smiled, feeling a little better about what I wanted to happen.

Sensing that, she said, "I'm kidding; that's my *real* husband."

Damn, nothing was going right so far; I could see my plan crumbling.

"It's like that," I said.

"Don't worry; he's leaving soon. He has to catch a red-eye flight," she said.

I nodded my head, and I don't know if that was her saying the ball is my in court or what. I wasn't about to let this opportunity pass me up.

"Okay, I'll see you later," I said.

"Mmmmh, if you can get away," she whispered, strutting away.

I could feel my dick getting hard. I was happy to play this little game with her. Now my mission was to send Candance's ass home. Before I could go looking for her, she was behind me, wrapping her arms around me.

"Hey, boo, I understand if you wanna go home, this shit is

kinda boring," I said.

"So, you're not going to come home with me?" she asked.

"Nah, you know I gotta stay. It's part of the job," I explained.

I hoped she would believe that.

"Well, I'm going to stay then." I smiled, but inside I was throwing a fit.

I kissed her forehead and told her that it was cool.

"I'm going to talk to some of my colleagues, so you go mingle," I said.

Before she could answer, I walked off. I spotted Naomi in the corner, smirking. I knew she thought this shit was funny. For the next twenty minutes or so, we both ended up in the same social circles.

"Mrs. Williams and Mr. Wright, you two do amazing work together. At the start of the year, there are a couple of accounts I want you both on," Mr. Cooper said.

Naomi eyed me and said, "I love working with Mr. Wright. We can make it happen."

It wasn't what she said but how she said it that made my dick hard. I could feel the precum sticking to my thigh.

"That's good to hear, now go enjoy the rest of the party."

She walked away before I could say anything to her, and I liked the fact she was playing hard to get. For the next forty-five minutes or so, we played this cat and mouse game. I was glad Candance started drinking because she began to loosen up. I'm pretty sure she wouldn't notice when I slipped off. Naomi's husband had finally left. Ten minutes later, she blew me a kiss and then slipped off down the hallway. I knew where she was going. I quickly found Candance and told her I was going to the bathroom.

"Okay, baby, take your time," she slurred.

I smiled and mumbled I plan too. I walked down the long corridor, took a right until I made it to the unisex restroom. I looked over my shoulder a couple of times to make sure nobody was following me. When I knew the coast was clear, I entered the restroom. I licked my lips as I watched her fix herself up in the mirror. I eased up behind her and kissed the nape of her neck.

"Damn, I've been waiting for this all night," I said.

"I'm glad you could finally getaway," she said.

We were looking at each other through the mirror.

"We gotta make this quick," I said.

"I know, we just fucking not making love," she stated.

I pulled her dress up over her hips and smacked her chocolate cakes.

"Why, you ain't got no panties on?" I asked, letting my fingers slip between her slick folds.

"I gave them to my husband," she smiled.

I grabbed her neck and licked the inside of her ear.

"Ooohh that feels so good," she moaned.

That made my dick harder.

"I know I said we had to make this quick, but I know this shit is too good to rush and bust," I said.

I pulled one of her titties out. They were so chocolate and perky. She pulled my fingers from between her legs and bought them up to her lips. We both watched in amazement at our reflections. She slowly turned around, and we faced each other and shared a nasty kiss. She skillfully unbuckled my belt and unzipped my pants.

"Ooohh, somebody is happy to see me," she said.

"You know he could be all yours," I said.

She smirked and kissed me again.

"We'll see about that. My husband's name is written all over my pussy."

Damn, she was so intoxicating, and I loved how she fluttered her thick lashes.

I smirked and said, "It must not be that good. If I got you in here with your dress over your hips, ready to risk it all."

She gave me a sly smile and pulled me closer by my tie. I leaned down to suck her nipples. She tasted good, and I couldn't help but lift her up in the air and smother my face between her thighs.

"Oh, my God! Calvin that feels so good," she said, grinding her pussy all over my face.

She tasted so good. Man, I wish I could take my time with her.

"Pretty lil' pussy," I moaned.

"Shit, that's enough, Calvin," she yelled.

Her legs were shaking, and her nails grazed my head. I sat her on top of the sink, and she was greedily licking all over my face. I loved kissing a woman after I ate her out. She was sucking on my chin and my lips.

"How you want it, baby?" I asked, moving my hand down my shaft.

"I want my legs in the crook of your arms while you hold

my wrist," she said, playing in her essence.

I pulled her to the edge of the counter, put her legs in the crook of my arms, and surprisingly, my joint slid right in. I threw my head back and pulled my bottom lip in.

"Got damn girl, you're lucky I got some control," I moaned.

"Yes, it feels so good," she moaned back.

For the first five minutes, I gave her my slow stroke to get her to open up a lil' more. I wanted her to beg for it. She's been playing hard to get all night, and I wanted her to know that I knew she had been feenin' for this good lovin'.

"Calvin, if you don't stop playing with me and fuck me," she groaned.

I started picking up the pace a lil' more, and I could feel my balls smack against her ass.

"Naomi, you got some good pussy, baby. I gotta get this shit from now on," I said.

"Daddy, you can have whatever you want," she said.

I pulled her up, so her titties were in my face, and I could control how much dick she was taking. She held me tighter and sucked my ear lobe in her mouth.

"Ooohh, the dick is better than I imagined. You got my cunt so wet."

I smacked her ass as I watched it jiggle in the mirror.

"You got my dick hard as shit."

She kissed me as I went deeper and deeper, hitting up against her spot.

"Calvin, don't stop. I'm almost there. You are about to make me cum."

I grabbed her wrist and started pounding away at her spot. I was enthralled with how her cream coated my dick. Right when I was about to pull out, her muscles tightened around me. I could feel my balls tighten.

"Fuck Naomi, I'm about to nut boo," I growled.

I quickly pulled out, and she got down on her knees and caught all of my nut. She didn't let a drop go to waste. I grabbed both sides of her head when she gently sucked on the tip.

"Fuck! I guess Christmas came early, huh?" I asked.

She laughed, "You are a mess."

She handed me some wet wipes, and we quickly got ourselves together. I grabbed some paper towels so I could dry my face.

"I enjoyed myself," she said.

"Yeah, that pussy is lethal. Imma want some more," I said, kissing her neck.

"Mmmpph, I see what I can make happen, but don't hold your breath. As I said, this belongs to my husband," she said, patting her pussy.

I stepped into her space and whispered in her ear, "You and I both know that's my pussy now."

We shared another kissed before leaving out the bathroom. I left out looking both ways to make sure nobody was lingering around. I made it back to the ballroom, and it looked like the party had hyped up. I scanned the area to see if I could find Candance. When I did, she was dancing her life away. I made my way over to her and grabbed her arm.

"Hey baby, how are you enjoying the party?" she asked.

Candance was drunk beyond her limit, so I knew she wouldn't remember me sneaking off.

"I'm enjoying it but let's get you home, boo. You're drunk as hell," I said.

I grabbed our coats and her purse and headed towards the double doors. I spotted Naomi talking to some higher-ups.

I overheard her say, "You know my work is never done. I had to check an email, and that turned into me sending some follow-up emails."

"That's why we keep you around, Mrs. Williams."

When she saw me, she smiled and said, "Have a good night and Happy Holidays, Mr. Wright."

I winked at her, walking out the double doors. Christmas had cum very early.

Nympho 15

Massage Therapy

I f you were to look up the word stress in the dictionary, you would see my face next to the definition. Now I know that's cliché, but it is so true! My life is full of stress. Stress from Grad School, stress from work, stress from life, stress from niggas, shit I'm stressing my damn self out talking about this shit. All I know is that a bitch needs a damn break.

My job was going on a two-week shutdown for the holidays, and I couldn't be more excited. I planned to relax, drink, smoke, sleep, and get some dick. The first plan of action was to get a full body massage. Back in September, I got myself a membership at a very elite spa and gym. I originally got it because I wanted to start working out, but that was a failed mission. I was paying $120 a month for an amenity I hadn't used in forever.

There was no time better than the present to schedule a massage, though. I was scrolling through their website and clicked on the spa tab. They had an abundance of massage options, but I needed something to relax and ease my stress. I decided on the XEN full body massage for 120 minutes.

I wanted to get my money's worth. I had the option to select my massage therapist, but I didn't care who it was as long as they were gentle with their hands. I pre-paid for the massage and scheduled it for December 23rd at 1:15 pm. I closed my computer counting down the days to my relaxation.

∞∞∞

Sunday...

It was a day before my appointment, and I was lying in my bed sulking. Because the nigga I was supposed to get some dick from decided he wanted to flake again. Of course, I could have called another one of my men, but out of all the other niggas I knew. Antonio had the best dick. Since I knew his ass wasn't coming, I decided to get myself off. Once I came, I rolled over and fell into a deep sleep, awaiting my massage.

∞∞∞

I woke up the next morning full of energy. I did some quick cleaning, cooked breakfast, and packed my gym bag because I wanted to get to the gym early and work out. I grabbed my keys and was on my merry way. It was about a 20-minute drive from my apartment to the gym. When I arrived, I headed to the locker room and changed into my workout clothes. I headed up to the workout floor and broke a sweat like a runaway slave.

2 hours later...

I was in the spa lobby, waiting for my massué. I was very relaxed. Glad I decided to get a little workout in before my massage. About five minutes passed before my massué came to the waiting room.

"Yes, she's right there," the receptionist said.

I grabbed my jacket and held my hand out for her to shake it.

"I'm Dee. I'll be your massage therapist today," she said.

I shook her hand and said, "Nice to meet you. I'm Zalani."

She licked her lips and said, "It is nice to meet you."

I can say that I am a woman who can appreciate a beautiful woman when I see one. I have never found myself sexually attracted to other women but got damn it; this girl was fine. Her masculine energy oozed from her pores, but I could tell she could be feminine when she wanted to be. As we walked, she asked me if I've had a professional massage before. I told her no.

"Then you're in for a real treat. Just let me know if you start to feel some painful pressure, and I'll ease up," Dee said.

"I definitely will," I said.

We walked into the large massage room. The ambiance was lovely; the lights were dim, meditation music played low, and burning incents swan around the room.

"So, I'm going to step out and let you undress. Undress to your comfort level. Some people get completely naked, some keep their underwear on, but it's up to you. Once you're done, ring the bell, and I'll be back," Dee explained.

"Okay, thank you," I said.

I decided to strip out of all my clothes. I folded them up nicely and placed them in the chair. I climbed up onto the memory foam massage table, and once I was comfortable, I rang the bell. Dee walked in. She took a seat at the head of the massage table and poured a generous amount of oil in her hands. She started at my shoulders and worked her fingers around my neck.

I couldn't believe how good her touch felt. Between my legs tingled, and my nipples hardened under the sheet.

"Damn, you are tense," she said.

"I know. I have a lot of stress in my life," I said.

"Well, for the next hour and fifty minutes, let all that stress go," she said.

I let my body fully relax, and when I did, I felt like I was floating. When she was done with my shoulders and neck, she started on my arms, but I peeped when she pulled the sheet down from my titties.

"Mmmpph," she mumbled.

She worked those magic fingers on my arms, but every so often, she would grab my breasts or tug at my nipples. When she did, I could feel my juices start to percolate. Her hands moved down to my stomach and traced the outline of my abs. She ran her fingers back up to my nipples, and she gently circled them.

"Oh my god," I moaned.

She smirked and asked, "You like that?"

I nodded my head, letting her know I was indeed enjoying her special massage. She worked on my titties for a good five minutes, and at this point, I wanted her to lean down and suck my nipples. But I wasn't that lucky.

"You can turn over on your stomach now," Dee said.

I rolled my eyes and turned over. She pulled the sheet down to the crack of my ass and poured warm oil all over my back. She used the palm of her hands to work my lower back. I was in pure bliss, and the sexual tension between us was suffocating. She began kneading all of the knots out of my back. Then she pulled the sheet from over my ass, and I made it jiggle a little bit.

"Damn," she whispered.

I smiled when she rubbed oil over my ass and started massaging it. She was trying to be subtle while copping feels, but I could tell she was getting carried away. I wanted Dee to make the first move. Every so often, she would spread my cheeks apart to expose my pussy and blow in my hole. Which caused my juices to spill out of me onto the sheets. All of a sudden, she ran her finger down the crack of my ass and into my pussy.

"Ooohh shit," I moaned.

"Damn you so wet," she said.

As she worked her fingers into me. She used her other hand to put it under my stomach to lift me up. I nearly lost my mind when her tongue snaked between my crack and into my pussy.

I wined my hips as she sucked on my clit like it was her favorite piece of candy. My eyes rolled to the back of my head as she continued to lick and suck on me. I can't remember ever getting head this good before. I couldn't put into words how amazing this shit felt. She smacked my ass as her tongue went deeper into my cunt.

"Fuck, you taste so good," Dee moaned.

"Mmmpph, and that tongue feel so good," I moaned back.

I was in pure bliss. I guess what they say is true; women can eat pussy, a lot better than men. I put both hands on my ass cheeks to spread them further apart, and Dee's tongue went deeper and deeper into my cunt. She licked the back of my thighs, causing a shiver to wrap its way around my spine. She bit and sucked on my cheeks before snaking her tongue in my asshole. She has my body on fire!

Before I could catch myself, I yelled out, "Fuck me!"

Dee stopped feasting on me, and I heard her smirk.

"How you wanna get fucked?" she asked, playing with my clit.

"On my back with my legs up over your shoulders," I whispered.

Dee smiled and then leaned down to kiss me. I hungrily sucked her tongue and chin, enjoying the taste of my juices. I felt like I was having an out-of-body experience. She sucked my earlobes, kissed my neck, then sucked on both of my nipples. She slipped her fingers back inside me.

"I wanna feel how tight that pussy gets while you're creaming," she whispered in my ear.

I moaned and said, "I'm tired of all this foreplay shit, fuck me."

She had this sinister smile on her face as she unzipped her pants and her strap on sprung out. I laughed.

"I take it you do this often?" I asked, using my fingers to replace hers.

She laughed and said, "Only the ones that I find sexy and freaky."

I pulled her down so I could kiss her. Our tongues were doing a sensual tango. In the middle of our passionate kissing, she slid her strap inside of me, and I swear it felt like I had the real thing gliding in me.

"Damn you so wet, girl," she moaned in my ear.

"Ooohh fuck, you feel so good, Dee," I sighed.

My eyes crossed when Dee leaned up, still stroking my walls, I pulled my bottom lip in. It felt so much better than the real thing. She licked her thumb and rubbed it gently across my swollen clit. This was some intense fucking.

"Oh, my fucking Gawd," I moaned.

If this is what sex is like with a woman, I had no problem switching teams.

"I knew you had some good pussy, the first time I saw you," she moaned.

I knew she was getting into it when she pulled her shirt behind her neck. I don't know why I was turned on, that she was flat-chested. I began to toy with her nipples, and grabbed her ass as she went deeper. I could feel my walls get tighter and tighter, but I was not ready to come yet.

"You are fucking me so good, Dee, but I want to ride it," I moaned.

"Oh yeah?" she asked.

"Oh yeah," I said.

She pulled out of me, and my cream dripped onto the sheets. I don't know what came over me, but I leaned down and started sucking it. I wanted to test the waters to see how turned-on Dee was. I slid my fingers between her legs, as I deep throated the plastic dick. She was almost as wet as me. I slid my pointer and middle finger into her hot hole.

"Yeah, yeah, Zalani. Damn baby, you are driving me crazy," she moaned.

I looked up at her, and she had her tongue curled over her top lip and her head thrown back in pure pleasure. We finally traded positions. She was lying on her back while I was on top. I eased down on the strap, and we both let out a moan. I still couldn't believe how good this felt. I leaned down so we could kiss as I popped my hips up and down. Her hands traveled from my wide hips down to my ass. She smacked it one cheek at a time.

"There you go, baby. Ride this dick," she moaned.

I was lost in a zone. I moaned as I slid my pussy up and down the strap.

I rode to the tip, then rode down the shaft. My juices spilled out of me and slid onto her fresh pussy lips. It turned me on, even more, knowing our juices were mingling together. I licked my fingers, reached behind me, and started playing with her pussy.

"Damn, girl, you so nasty," she said.

I was enjoying every minute of this. I was riding her as if my life depended on it. My titties bounced up and down, and I could feel my thighs burning. I continued to work her pussy.

"Dee, I want you to cum for me. I want us to cum together," I moaned.

"We gon' nut together, baby," she said.

She leaned forward and wrapped her arms around my back and started sucking on my nipples and licking all over my neck.

"Oh, my God! Dee, it feels so good. Mmmpph, I think I'm about to cum," I moaned.

I rode faster until I was hitting my spot.

"Ooohh, I feel it, Lani, that's your spot, huh?" Dee asked, kissing my neck.

I pulled my fingers from her pussy, and we both took turns licking my fingers clean. My brows knitted together, I pulled my bottom lip in and dug my nails into her back. My pussy started to spasm as I felt my orgasm invade my entire body.

"Ooohh shit! I am about to fucking cum!" I yelled.

No sooner had the words left my mouth I was cumming, and the timer was going off, letting us know my massage was over. I threw my head back to catch my breath, but Dee was still kissing all over me.

"Did you enjoy yourself?" she asked.

"Enjoyment is an understatement; that was fucking amazing," I said.

She placed a kiss on my lips, then sucked my nipples.

"Imma step out and let you get cleaned up," she said.

I nodded my head and watched as she pulled off her strap-on, sprayed some cleaner on it, and wiped my juices off. Once she left, I took a seat in the chair. Damn, I can't believe that happened. I honestly felt more relaxed than I did coming here. I put my clothes back on and met Dee out in the hallway. We smiled at each other.

"I hope you have a great rest of your day, and please *cum* back," she said once we made it to the front.

"Thank you for the wonderful massage, and I will be coming back very soon," I said.

I watched as Dee walked out of the waiting room. I felt my panties becoming moist as I thought about our little secret. I walked out of the gym, floating on a cloud. My first girl on girl experience was one I would never forget.

Nympho 16

The New Exec Pt. II

I was sitting in my office, horny as hell, stroking my dick through my slacks. I couldn't stop thinking about that day in Shantél's office. That girl kept me turned on, and what made me want her even more, is the fact that she acted like nothing ever happened between us. I needed her right now! I unbuckled my belt, unzipped my pants, and then watched as my pipe sprung from its hiding place. My hand moved slowly up & down my length. I spit in my hand, so it felt like I was pumping into a hot, wet pussy. My mind wandered off to that day in her office. I remember walking in on her and them pretty long; legs splayed wide open.

The sweet smell of her pussy traveled to my nostrils. My dick immediately got harder. I licked my lips as I remembered how her nectar tasted, coating my tongue. My hand moved faster around my dick. My nasty thoughts were interrupted when my office phone buzzed.

"Yes!" I yelled into the intercom.

"Hi Mr. Williams, it's Miss Baker," she said into the receiver.

Her voice alone made me ooze pre-cum.

"What do you need?" I asked.

"I have a few documents that need your signature. When's a good time to come, see you?" she asked.

A smile crept up on my face as I told her now is perfect.

"Okay, see you in 10."

With that, she hung up, and I continued to stroke my pipe. Five minutes later, Shantél walked her fine ass into my office.

"Oh my god!" she yelled, trying to hide her smile.

I stuffed my dick back in my slacks and walked over to her, and whispered, "Don't be scared, baby."

I kissed her neck and gently pushed her against the door.

"I don't think we should do this," she moaned.

I was already unbuttoning her blouse and pulling the straps of her bra down.

"Stop acting like you don't want me pippin' you out," I said, nibbling on her nipples.

I was glad when she finally gave in and wrapped her hands around my dick.

"I haven't stopped thinking about that day in my office," she moaned.

"You could have fooled me, baby, because every time you walk by me, you act like nothing ever happened," I said.

"Well, I am in a relationship," she said, kissing me.

I knew whoever Shantél's man is, is a lucky muthafucka. This time she didn't have on a skirt, so that pussy wasn't easily accessible.

"Tony, I want you to eat my pussy," she whispered.

"I got you, baby."

I kissed a trail down to her stomach and slowly unfastened her black slacks. She had on a red lace thong, which her juices had already soaked. I put her smooth mocha legs over my shoulders and proceeded to bury my face in her crotch.

"Ooohh Tony, that feels so good," she moaned.

I loved eating pussy. I could have Shantél's for breakfast, lunch, and dinner. I pulled her thong to the side and went to work on that clit.

"Dayum! You taste so good girl," I moaned into her pussy.

"Your tongue feels so good, but I want some dick," she said, trying to climb down.

I opened her legs wider and buried my face in her thighs.

"Nigga I'm about to come!" She yelled.

I wanted her to bust her first nut in my mouth so she would be ready for this beat down I was about to give her. I didn't realize how turned on I was until I felt my nut slid down my thigh. She yelled as her essence coated my tongue.

I wrapped her legs around my waist and fed her my long tongue. Nothing turned me on more than a woman tasting her juices.

"I want you to hit it from the back again," she said into my neck.

"Nah baby, I want you on your back," I said.

As we walked to my desk, I held her big, juicy ass in my hands. Before I laid her on her back, I knocked all my files over.

"I can't wait to feel that big dick in my tight cunt," she said.

She leaned back, guiding my hard-on into her wetness. We both gasped as her wetness engulfed me. I leaned my tall frame over her and grabbed the corners of my desk as I started stroking. I watched as she leaned forward and licked my nipple.

"Fuck, you feel so good inside me," she moaned.

I kissed her as her walls wrapped tighter around me. I decided I wanted to tip drill. So, I pulled all the way out and just kept the tip in, Shantél had her eyes closed tight, and her bottom lip pulled in.

"You like this dick, baby?" I asked.

"Yes!" She yelled.

Then I pulled out several times and smacked my meat against her swollen clit.

"Tony quit playing and put that dick back in me," Shantél groaned.

I smiled and slid back into her. I was giving her my swimmers stroke and playing with that clit.

"Tell me this my pussy," I growled.

"It's your pussy, daddy."

I started to pound on that spot, and her eyes crossed, and she dug her nails into my back. I pounded harder and deeper on her spot until she couldn't take it anymore. Her walls wrapped viciously around my dick, and her nails dug deeper into my back.

"Oh, my Gawd! I'm about to cum, Tony!" She yelled.

I looked down as her pussy skeeted and covered my dick in her cream. I pulled out, and she quickly pushed me into my chair, got down on her knees, and greedily sucked my pipe into her mouth. Now it was my turn to act like a little bitch. My eyes were closed tight, and I could feel my nut build up in my balls.

"Fuck, girl!" I growled as my dick pushed past her tonsils.

Before I knew it, I was busting a river load down her throat. She kept sucking on my already sensitive head until I was busting another nut. She pulled my dick from her throat and smacked it across her full, pouty lips.

"Are you ready to sign those papers?" She asked, laughing.

A satisfied smile made its way across my face as I leaned back in my chair. Damn, that nut felt good!

Nympho 17

The Cable Guy

After living with my parents for the last three and a half years, I was ecstatic to have my own place and privacy. Don't get me wrong; I was grateful to stay with my parents because it allowed me to save my coins and be in the position, I'm in now. But I couldn't take the nagging, micro-managing, and trying to get some dick was a hassle in itself.

One my pussy needed to feel a hard dick at least 3-4 times a week. Secondly, I was tired of fucking niggas in the backseat of their cars. Don't get me wrong, I'm all for a surprise pulling over on the side of the road, and pulling my panties to the side but doing that shit on the regular was whack and played out. I had just gotten out of the shower, and I was bumping Ari Lennox's: *New Apartment.* That shit was speaking to my soul. I dropped my towel from around my body and started to wind my waist.

I was lost in my own world, running my hands through my hair and over my breast. I was debating if I wanted to call one of my fuck buddies over. I decided against it. I didn't want anyone to know where I lived just yet. I was startled out of my thoughts because somebody was knocking on my door like the police.

"Who is it?" I yelled.

"It's Direct Tv to install your cable," he answered.

Fuck! I mumbled under my breathe. I forgot they were coming out today.

"Okay, hold on!" I yelled back.

I ran to my room and threw on the first thing I could find. Then I rushed back into the living room to answer the door.

"Sorry about that, you can come in," I said.

I opened the door for him to come in and I was pleasantly surprised by how handsome the cable guy is.

"My bad, I'm late. I was stuck in traffic," he said.

I looked down at his name tag; it read Mac.

"No problem... Mac. I forgot y'all were coming out today," I said.

I moved aside to let him in. His lusty gaze heated my mocha skin. I watched as he walked in with his bag of tools.

"What rooms am I installing the cable in?" He asked.

"Just the living room," I said.

"Okay, cool," he said.

He bent down and started to grab his tools.

"Let me know if you need anything," I said.

"Aiight," he looked up, eyeing me.

$\infty\infty\infty$

2 hours later...

I was sitting at my island doing some work and grading papers. I was slightly irritated because this nigga was still here. I got up and took a seat on the arm of the couch.

"How much longer is this going to be?" I asked.

He looked at me, licked his lips, and said, "My bad, I just got done training a couple of days ago, and this is my first time doing this."

I sucked my teeth and rolled my eyes. Once I took a good look at him, my panties melted off me. He was tall; he wasn't overly muscular and not too skinny, more like a slim build. His bald head was smooth and shiny, his goatee was neatly trimmed, making his full brown lips look more luscious. He had these gigantic hands that I could only imagine grabbing my ass like Spalding basketballs. He wore tiny, gold hoop earrings that set his look off right. Mmmpph, he had my pussy puckering, and I wanted a taste of him.

"My bad, I wanna be outta your space, as bad as you want me out," he said.

His deep voice snapping me out of my nasty thoughts. At that moment, I realized I had been a bitch.

"I'm sorry," I said.

He pulled his bottom lip in and said, "You good, baby."

I hid my smile, got up from the couch, and leaned against the wall.

"Where is your man?" He asked.

He was trying his best not to look at my hardened nipples.

I smirked and said, "I don't have a man."

He smiled. That smile let me know he was ready for something to pop off. I wasn't sure if I should make the first move or let him do it. We were both staring each other down, waiting to see who was going to cave first. I slid the straps of my tank top down my shoulders to let my titties bounce and sway. Mac licked his lips, dropping the remote and running his hand over his hard-on. I lifted both my ta-ta's and flicked my tongue across my nipples. Lust swam in his pupils as he hungrily watched me play with my titties.

"Dayum baby, that shit is sexy," he said.

He began to slowly make his way towards me. As he got closer, I lifted my right leg so that he could wrap it around his waist. In one swift motion, he had my back pressed against the wall, pressing his hard body into mine. My pussy was on fire. I just hoped and prayed that he knew how to use his pipe. He licked and sucked on my neck. Then he took his huge hands and lifted my titties so that he could suck on them. My eyes rolled to the back of my head as he slowly flicked his tongue across my hard nipples. My nails grazed the back of his head.

"Shit, that feels so good, boy," I moaned.

He stopped sucking my nipples, kissed my neck and chin. Then he used his tongue to spread my lips. We shared a hungry, passionate kiss, making my pussy wetter. I could feel his dick start to pitch a tent in his navy-blue khakis.

"You want this pussy, don't you?" I asked.

I seductively nipped at his earlobe.

He smiled and said, "Hell yeah! I wanted it since I walked up in this muthafucka."

I giggled as he carried me over to my couch. I used my right foot to caress his hard-on.

"Hold them legs up," he demanded.

I gladly lifted my long shapely legs, so my shorts wedged between my ass and cunt. Making my pussy look fatter.

"Dayum! This pussy looks so good," he moaned.

I excitedly watched as he spanked my twat, then kneeled between my legs and deeply inhaled. He began to lick and suck on my inner thighs, kissing my calves and then sucking both of my big toes into his mouth. My eyes rolled up in my head as I rubbed his head.

I tried to pull my shorts over my hips, but he grabbed both of my wrists and said, "Nah, leave'em on and pull'em to the side."

He looped his long, slender fingers in between the crotch of my shorts and pulled them to the side as far as they could go. He inhaled my scent before sticking his tongue out and gently licking my clit.

"Oh my god," I moaned.

I arched my back and wined my hips in his face. I laid my hand on his forehead to push him away.

"What are you running for? Let daddy eat this pussy," he

said.

He pushed my legs back further. I bit my lip, and my body continued to lift off the couch. His spit and my juices mingled together, sliding down the crack of my ass and staining my couch.

"Fuck, that feels so good," I moaned, cradling the back of his head.

"Mmppph, you taste good," Mac said.

I couldn't remember the last time I've gotten head so good. I toyed with my nipples as Mac continued to feast on me.

"Stick your tongue in my pussy," I said.

He happily obliged, using his fingers to rub on my clit.

"Oh, my Gawd, I'm about to cum," I said.

"Nah, don't cum yet, baby. I want all that sweet cream on my dick."

I smiled, pushing him away from me. I slid to the edge of the couch and caressed his ever-growing pipe. He entangled his fingers into my hair.

He said, "I hope you know how to use them pretty lips."

I smirked because he was in for a treat. No matter how much shit niggas talked, as soon as they hit the bottomless pit, I called my throat; they were nutting off in seconds. I looked up into his lust-filled eyes and smiled at him. I slowly unzipped his pants, and his dick sprung from his boxers, bouncing up & down. My mouth watered at the beautiful masterpiece, and my pussy throbbed. Mac had a huge mushroom head; it was long and thick, very well portioned. My Gawd! He had the balls to match. I puckered my lips together and nestled his head between them. His sticky nectar was already dripping onto my tongue.

"Ooohh shit, baby, gone 'head and slide all that meat in your mouth," he moaned.

I ignored him and massaged his balls as I continued to tease the head. There was nothing I loved more than sucking dick, and right now, the deepest part of my soul was being satsified. I began to inch him deeper and deeper down my throat. Soft moans escaped from his lips the deeper he went. When he realized his balls were hitting against my chin and I wasn't gagging, his knees buckled.

"Fuck, baby! You are a pro, girl; I ain't ever had my dick sucked like this before," he moaned fucking my face.

There was a long stream of spit that dripped from my mouth onto my rug. I continued to massage his heavy nuts as I gobbled up his tasty meat. I knew he was right at the edge when he grabbed my head tighter and fucked my throat like it was my pussy. I pulled him from my never-ending throat. He had this glassy look in his eyes, and I was mesmerized by how he was jacking off.

He smiled at me and said, "You about to get it."

He leaned down and kissed me. I got up and straddled the arm of the couch. My skin heated up when he rubbed his strong hands over my round ass. He smacked it so hard that it caused my arch to go deeper and my clit to throb. He pulled my ass cheeks apart and buried his face deep in my pussy.

"Pretty ass pussy," he moaned.

"Boy, stop playing and fuck me," I groaned.

"I'm ready to get knee-deep in this gushy," he said, sandwiching himself between my ass cheeks.

He pulled my hair from my face and fed me his pussy and ass-stained tongue. My scent was intoxicating, and I couldn't take this teasing shit anymore.

"Mac quit playing and give me that dick," I said.

He smiled, pulled me to the edge of the armrest, and kissed the nape of my neck. Mac palmed both of my cheeks and spat in between them. Then he guided his head into me. I gasped as he eased into me. I was tight and wet.

"There you go, baby. Take that dick boo," he said.

I bit my bottom lip until I knew all of him was in me.

"Ooohh, you feel so good daddy," I moaned.

He started grinding into me nice and slow so that I could get used to his length and girth. Once I got open for him, this nigga was hitting the bottom of my pussy.

"Ooohh nigga, that's it! Fuck this pussy!" I growled.

His balls smacked the back of my pussy, causing me to cream harder.

"This sweet pussy taking this pipe so good girl. I knew this na-na was gone be pressure," he moaned into my ear.

I smiled, lifted-up a little bit, and started to throw this ass back on that dick. I was riding his dick so good, he gripped my hips tighter, so he would be in control. He smacked ass so hard; it made my cunt grow wetter. He wrapped his hands around my neck and long stroked me.

My eyes rolled to the back of my head. He licked the side of my neck and gently bit it.

"Boo, you gotta let me have this pussy from now on. You ain't giving this pussy to nobody but me, this my shit now..."— he paused— "You creaming all on my dick."

He was driving me crazy; I couldn't even think straight.

"Yeeeeeesssss daddy, it's yours, it's all yours!" I yelled.

He started smacking my ass harder; once he let me take control, I was twerking this ass all on him. I was ready to talk my shit.

"Stick your thumb in my ass," I said.

He smirked and happily obliged.

"Freaky ass," he said.

I alternated between clapping my ass and slow wining on his long pipe.

"This your pussy nigga? You are fucking me so good," I groaned.

"You taking this dick like a pro, baby," he moaned.

He grabbed my hips and started pounding on my spot. He pulled my hair, causing me to snap my neck back. He gave me his tongue again and toyed with my nipples. I arched my back deeper because I knew he was close to nutting.

"Stay just like that. I'm about to nut all in that pussy," he growled.

I kept wining my hips as my orgasm swam through my body. Shortly after I was coming, he was too.

"Aahhh shit! Fuck! Baby, that's it; take that nut!" He yelled.

Mac pulled out of me and smacked my ass again. His nut felt so good inside me.

"Push it out."

I pushed our nuts out of me. He rubbed his thumb on my asshole, then leaned down to kiss it and stick his tongue in my creamy cunt.

"Nasty nigga," I moaned.

I rolled off the armrest onto my back. He leaned down and shared the fruits of our labor with me.

"Dayum! Imma need your name and your number," he said.

I laughed and said, "I'm Natalie."

"Nice to meet you, Natalie," he said.

We both started laughing.

"You know you were my last appointment for the day," he said.

I smiled and said, "Well, I'm glad I didn't put you in jeopardy of losing your job."

I was still lying on my back. His dick was slowly growing harder.

He leaned down, kissed my neck, and said, "I'm trying to clock out and fuck again."

I ran my tongue over his thick lips and grinded my hips into him.

"Then, let's fuck," I said guiding his hard-on back inside of me.

121

Nympho 18

Peeping Jamal

I've been called many names from a pervert, dirty dog, creep, and so many more derogatory terms come to mind. But I like to think of myself as a voyeur. I loved nothing more than watching people have sex, whether they knew I was there or not. I don't know if it was the thrill of being caught or the fact most people didn't think I was there. Man, it was something about watching two people in the heat of the moment, unaware of what's around them, that made my dick harder than Chinese arithmetic. Now that I'm standing here thinking about this kink, of mine, it started way back when I was in college.

My sophomore year of college, I decided to get a roommate to help offset the rent. Shorty was a cool lil' chick, stayed to herself, and minded her business. But baby girl liked to get fucked! Every other day there was a new nigga blowing her back out. I remember coming home from class early one afternoon, and as usual, she had a friend over. I ignored the moaning and groaning for as long as I could. But curiosity had gotten the best of me. I walked to her door, hoping I could hear them more clearly. But the door was cracked, just enough for me to peek through. Once I got a *clear view of the action; I couldn't pull myself away. It was like my feet were glued to the floor.*

Common sense had flown out the window when I reached into my joggers and pulled my dick out. I was caught up in the moment that I hadn't realize my roommate was staring at me. I jumped back at first, but when I noticed she was cool with me watching, our party was on and popping. To this day, I don't know what made her leave that door cracked, but I'm glad she did. We never had sex, but it was our unspoken rule. Whenever she was getting fucked, she always made sure to leave the door cracked so I could get my peek on.

∞∞∞

I loved where my apartment was located; the complex was shaped in a circle. So, depending on where you lived in the complex, people could get a good look at someone's daily routine. My apartment was situated in the sweet spot; I could see into four or five apartments if I wanted to. There was this fine ass brown sista who lived directly across from me, and I had a perfect view into her bedroom.

She reminded me a lot of my roommate; she always had a new nigga beating that pussy up. I loved watching that shit. I knew I was obsessed with her; I usually don't want to fuck the women I watch, but with her, I couldn't wait to be knee-deep in that wet-wet.

We always played this lil' game with each other. She would leave the curtains to her bedroom open so people could get their peep show on. I remember our first inter-action happened a couple months ago.

She asked me if I watched her have sex, and of course, I lied about it. I knew, she knew I was lying, but she didn't push it. From that point on, she gave me my little shows, and we've watched each other masturbate.

As many times as I've watched her get fucked. I'm pretty sure she's watched my pipework too. Right now, I'm standing in the middle of my room, with my dick in my hand stroking it, watching her get on her knees.

"There you go, baby, suck that dick," I moaned.

I could tell she was a pro. She bobbed up and down on the dude's shaft while massaging his balls.

"Yeah, lick them balls boo," I moaned again.

I looked down, and there was pre-cum everywhere. I was moving my hips like I was the one getting sucked off. I could tell dude had enough, because he pushed her away and motioned for her to get on the bed. I looked on in excitement as he pulled her hair back and smacked her ass. I continued to look through my binoculars, and my dick got harder as we made eye contact. I moved my hand faster up and down my lengthy shaft.

We kept our eyes locked on each other, and just as my nut gushed out of me, she blew me a kiss.

Three days later...

I was down in the mail center, checking to see if I had any packages, when I bumped into an ole girl.

"Pay attention to where you are going next time," she said.

I smiled and said, "My bad."

She stared me up & down and said, "Hold on."

She motioned for me to come closer.

"What's up?" I asked.

"I'm Amber," she said.

"I'm Jamal," I said.

We both looked at each other, letting our nasty thoughts evade us.

"I know I asked you this already, but I know you like watching me get fucked," she stated.

I blushed, not sure what to say.

"I'm not mad at you, but make sure you're ready for this weekend. I have a very special treat for you," she explained.

I laughed and said, "Aiight."

She stepped into me and kissed my cheek before walking away. I smiled. I don't know what Amber had in mind, but a nigga was ready to find out. I knew she had to be lethal in the bedroom. Being in her presence made me leak pre-cum. I rushed back to my apartment, so I could bust this nut.

So, for the next few days, we played this tit-for-tat game with each other. One night, I watched while she masturbated. The next night she watched, while I sexed one of my fuck buddies. The following night we had phone sex, making each other come long and hard. The weekend was fast approaching, and I couldn't wait to find out what Amber had planned.

Saturday evening...

I was oiling my body as I looked out my colossal bay windows to see Amber setting up her apartment. I walked over to my bed and opened the box that Amber dropped off yesterday. There was lube, a fleshlight, a cock ring, and a camera. I laid all my goodies on my bed ,when a note fell out of the box.

It read: *I hope you're ready for what's in store tonight. You won't have to worry about being uncomfortable. Hook up the camera for your live show. The party starts at 9. XOXOXO.* I smirked.

This girl was something else. I looked down at my watch; it was 8:55. I hurriedly went over to my tv, to get the camera set up. Once I did, I had an amazing view of Amber's bedroom. I smiled when she took a seat in front of her camera and took a sip of her wine.

"I'm glad you could join me, daddy," she said.

"No problem, what's with the setup? I was cool watching through my window," I said.

"I wanted you to be comfortable," she said.

I nodded my head, and I could feel my dick start to stretch along my thigh. Before I could say anything, there was a knock at her door. I was smiling like a kid at Christmas, when two women walked in.

I'm a lucky muthafucka, I thought to myself. I watched as Amber kissed both women and told them to undress. They all had ass and titties out of this world.

"Ladies, my little peeping Tom is right here," she said, pointing at the screen.

They both looked at me, smiling.

"He's cute," one of them said.

"I told him he was in for a real treat."

"He is," the other said rubbing her titties.

My dick sprung from my towel, and it seemed to be getting harder by the minute. I grabbed the bottle of lube and poured a generous amount over my pipe. I watched excitedly as they moved closer and kissed each other.

"Ooohh shit," I moaned.

I moved my hand up and down my dick as pre-cum oozed from the head. They began to pour oil all over each other and rub their titties together. I learned that the other shorties' names were Tasha and Camille. Tasha laid on her back while Camille went to sit on her face.

Amber lifted Tasha's legs up, kissed her thighs and pulled out this extra-long black dildo, and started fucking Tasha.

"Aahhh shit, y'all got a nigga hard as fuck over here," I moaned.

I watched intently as Tasha ate Camille's pussy, and Amber ate and fucked Tasha. I moved my hand faster up and down my shaft.

"Fuck, I think I'm about to bust," I said.

"Don't cum yet, daddy. We haven't even gotten started yet. Put the cock ring on," Camille said.

I happily obliged. My balls felt heavy, and I knew I was going to be popping a huge nut.

"You like watching us fuck each other?" Amber asked.

"Hell yeah," I moaned.

I used my right hand to stroke my joint nice, and slow and used my left hand to play with my nipple.

"How that pussy taste?" I asked.

They mumbled good. Amber climbed on top of Tasha and started sucking on Camille's nipples, while Tasha put the dildo inside of Amber.

"Ooohh fuck Tasha that feels so good," Amber moaned.

Amber sucked on Camille's titties while Tasha fucked Amber. This shit was so hot, and I wished I was there, so I could smell all of their aroma's. Camille finally climbed off Tasha and leaned down to kiss her. Then all three of them started kissing.

"Damn," I whispered.

Amber bent over and put that arch in her back, Camille took the dildo and started fucking herself with it, and Tasha started eating Amber from the back.

"Y'all so fucking nasty yo," I moaned.

"Yes, Tasha! You always eat my pussy so good," Amber moaned.

"You always taste so good," Tasha moaned back.

Then Camille turned her attention to me and said, "I know you're close, but you gotta slow down."

She told me to stroke slower.

"Don't focus on nutting and bring your attention to the moment," she instructed.

Once I did that, the sensations intensified.

"Damn yo, this feels so good," I moaned.

Camille got up and traded places with Tasha, and she put the dildo into Amber's ass and started eating her out. Tasha laid at the edge of the bed, and exposed her pretty pink pussy, and slipped her fingers inside.

"How you like watching us fuck each other, daddy?" Tasha asked.

"I love that shit," I said.

"Oh, my God! I'm about to come," Amber moaned.

Once Amber got her nut off, all three of them laid on their backs, and all of them had their own dildos.

"Grab your fleshlight, baby," Amber said.

I grabbed the fleshlight and poured more lube on myself, then eased it down my pipe like it was a real cunt. My eyes rolled to the back of my head. This felt just like the real thing. They all started playing with themselves. Our apartments turned into a moan fest.

"Y'all are so sexy. I wish I could feel all that pussy," I moaned.

"Daddy, we wish you were here to fuck us," Tasha moaned.

Amber climbed on top of Camille, overlapping one thigh over the other. They began to rub their clits against each other.

"Oh, my God! Amber, you know this is my favorite position," Camille moaned.

Tasha leaned over and started sucking on their titties and smacking Amber's ass. I was glad they were facing me cause that shit looked good as hell. I pumped faster into the mold, and I could feel my balls tighten up.

"Y'all know how to drive a nigga crazy. Fuck I want to cum down y'all's throat," I moaned.

"Yes, cum for us, baby. We want that nut daddy," Tasha said.

Amber and Camille were moaning and groaning about how they were about to cum. As Amber climbed off Camille, she started squirting.

I got a couple of quick pumps in, and I pulled the flesh-light off, and my nut shot up to ceiling. It was on my stomach, chest, chin, and lip. I licked it up.

"That was so fun," they said in unison.

"Hell yeah, next time I cumming in some pussy," I said, falling back onto my bed.

They all laughed and promised it would happen next time.

Nympho 19

Couple's Retreat Pt. II

The Next Day...

I'm not sure if Selena sensed that something went down between Keni and I, last night, but I hadn't seen her all day. After Keni sucked the skin off my dick, I decided to sleep on the couch. When I woke up this morning, Selena wasn't in our room. Every time I would ask Keni if she'd seen Selena, she would say no, but then it was always accompanied by a weird ass smile. My mind began getting the best of me because I hadn't seen Tyree all morning either. My racing thoughts were put at ease when Tyree walked into the room.

"What's up, man?" he asked.

I gave him a head nod and tried calling my wife again. When she didn't answer, I slammed my hands on the counter. When I looked up to ask Tyree if he had seen Selena. He was nowhere to be found.

I walked outside and asked, "C'mon Keni, where is Selena?"

She looked over at me and said, "She went to the connecting cabin. It's a bunch of other amenities there."

"Thank you," I said.

I went to put on some tennis shoes and began my trek to the other cabin.

15 minutes later...

I walked in the front door and was immediately impressed with the connecting cabin. Shit, I liked this more than the main cabin. I was trying to find a bathroom cause a brotha had to piss. I rushed to the first room that looked like it could have been a bathroom. I knocked on the door first, and when nobody answered, I went to open it. When I realized what was going on, I smiled. I backed out to give them some privacy, but as I looked up again. I noticed it was my wife and Tyree. I was frozen in place. Not that I had a right to be mad, considering Keni had my dick down her throat last night. I was still hurt. Selena had her head thrown back with her bottom lip pulled in.

"Oh my god, Tyree, you feel so good," she moaned.

"You feel better baby," Tyree moaned back.

I was trying to leave, but I couldn't. Although I was mad, I was enthralled by what was happening. Selena had one leg propped on the sink while her hands tightly grasped both sides of it.

"There you go, baby! You look so fucking sexy taking this dick," Tyree groaned.

I can't remember the last time Selena looked to be in ecstasy when we fucked.

"Daddy, you are fucking me so good," she moaned, making my dick hard.

Tyree smiled and said, "I wanted you for so long, girl."

Selena's eyes rolled to the top *of* her head. All I could see were the whites of her eyes, but I peeped Ty looking at me through the mirror. He had a sly grin plastered on his face. I continued to watch in anger and excitement as he fucked my wife. My hand moved into my jogging pants, and I began stroking myself. **Selena began to throw it back, matching Tyree's rhythm.**

"Yes, Daddy, that big dick is making my pussy cream. Fuck me nigga."

Tyree kissed her neck and wrapped her ponytail around his fist.

"I love how you taking it," he moaned.

Selena had a towel around her neck, and Tyree wrapped it around his hands. Then he pulled it some to choke her.

"Oh my god! Ty, that's my spot," Selena groaned.

The sounds of his balls smacking against the back of my wife's pussy were turning me on. Tyree put his left leg up on the sink to dig deeper into Selena. He was balls deep in my wife.

"Fuck this pussy nigga!" she yelled.

He smacked her ass so hard that it echoed throughout the hallway.

"Fuck, girl! You gon' make me nut," Ty moaned.

"Mmmpph, I want you to nut to inside me."

I bit my lip. I was too turned on to be pissed.

"Don't tell me that, Selena," he said.

She looked back at him and smiled. He put his leg down and leaned into Selena.

They shared a sloppy kiss.

"I wanna bust on that pretty face," he whispered.

"I got you daddy," she panted.

I didn't know if I wanted to stay to see the grand finale. She damn sho' never let cum on her face before.

"God...dayum, I'm about to nut!" Tyree yelled.

He quickly pulled out, and Selena got down on her knees. His nut gushed on her face. Selena had cum dangling from her eyelashes and nose. I watched as she licked it from her lips.

"Ooohh, you taste so good," she moaned.

He leaned down to kiss her, and he said, "Damn, I'm ready to get 'round two on and popping. Let's go to the bedroom."

"I got you, daddy."

I quickly pulled my sweats up and raced to the front door. Before they could catch me. I couldn't believe I let another man fuck my wife and just sat back and watched.

Dumbass, I thought to myself.

Later that week...

Surprisingly me and Selena had some breakthroughs in our relationship. I'm not sure if Selena knows what went down between me and Keni. But she hadn't mentioned a word about it. I hadn't mentioned her little fuck session with Tyree either. I was on the lower balcony smoking a cigar when Tyree came out. I rolled my eyes. I don't know how to feel about this brotha.

"What's up, dawg?" he asked.

I gave him a nod, and went back to minding my business.

He laughed and asked, "Marcus, what is your problem? You've been acting real, funny style lately."

I ashed my cigar and said, "Ain't nothing wrong with me, dawg."

"Man, if you got a problem with me being bi-sexual, just say that," he said.

"You a grown-ass man. Do what makes you happy playa..." –I paused taking a deep inhale— "How did that shit happen anyway?" I asked.

He lit a blunt and explained, "Long story short; Keni and I were having one of our buddies over, and I got caught up in the heat of the moment. I tried it a few more times to see if what I was feeling was true, and here I am."

I shook my head. I still couldn't believe this shit. He passed me the blunt, and I took a couple of puffs. Getting lost in my own world.

"Did you plan to fuck my wife?" I finally asked.

He smirked, "Ain't this the pot calling the kettle black. Don't act like Keni didn't have your dick down her throat."

I smacked my lips and said, "Coming on this trip was a mistake."

Tyree blew out a cloud of smoke and said, "Dawg, you got to live a little. Stop being so damn uptight. I guarantee you, your prudeness is why Selena has shut down."

I squinted my eyes and asked, "What the hell is that supposed to mean?"

He laughed. "Selena ain't the woman you think she is," he

explained.

I was still lost, trying to figure out what this nigga was talking about. My confusion was evident on my face.

"Follow me," he said, putting out the blunt.

I followed him around the balcony. He stopped in front of someone's bedroom and opened the door.

"I ain't got time for this," I said.

"Damn shut up and listen for once," Tyree said.

From a distance, I saw Keni and Selena both wrapped in towels. What piqued my curiosity is when Selena leaned into Keni, and they kissed.

"Your wife's bi-sexual Marcus," Tyree said.

This trip had been full of surprises. I had so many questions, but my throbbing dick was already thinking for us. Tyree started walking, and I quickly followed his lead. We walked into another massive bedroom.

I heard Keni say, "Now I'm going to pay you back for all the wonderful head you use to give me."

I couldn't believe my wife was a certified freak. We both stopped in our tracks and watched in excitement as our wives kissed each other. They unwrapped each other's towels, and Selena leaned back into the pillows. Keni sucked on her nipples, kissed her stomach, then smiled at her sticky treat.

"I have waited so long to taste you," Keni said, sliding her fingers into my wife.

I was caught in a daze. I've enjoyed lesbian porn but to be able to witness it in person was mesmerizing.

"Oh my god, Keni, that feels so good," my wife moaned.

Out the corner of my eye, I peeped Tyree taking his clothes off. I pulled my shorts down and spat in my hand and started stroking my hard-on. Keni was going in on that pussy. She pushed Selena's legs back further, and her tongue snaked between her pussy and ass.

"There you go, baby. Eat that pussy, Keni," Tyree said.

Keni moaned louder while eating out my wife. My dick was oozing pre-cum. I tried to walk over to the bed, but Keni made a hand gesture, and Tyree pulled me back.

"Stay right here, dawg. Enjoy the show," he said.

I rolled my eyes, but my balls tingled at the lovely sight in front of me. I watched as Tyree slowly jacked his dick off. I ain't know what was going on. But my mind was racing with a bunch of freaky thoughts. I slowed my rhythm down so that I wouldn't nut yet. We both watched as Keni pushed Selena's legs into a split. Keni put her right leg over Selena's, and they started grinding their pussies against each other. Man, that shit looked so sexy.

"Oh my god! I forgot how good this feels," Selena moaned.

She pulled Keni down so they could kiss.

"Damn, y'all look so fucking good," I sighed.

Their wet pussies echoed throughout the room. I looked over at Tyree, and he was fucking into his fist as if it were a hot, wet throat. I don't know what came over me, but as our wives, yelled they were cumming. I reached over and wrapped my hand around Ty's dick.

"Oh, shit, yo! You good Marcus?" he asked.

I nodded my head and stroked both of our dicks. Selena had her eyes glued on me, smiling.

"Stand in front of each other and rub y'all's dicks against each other," Selena demanded.

We happily obliged. I wrapped both my hands around our pipes as we slid in and out of my palms.

"Damn, this feels good," I moaned.

I pulled my bottom lip in as Tyree continued to glide in and out of my hand. He wrapped his hand around my neck and pulled my head to his. Our foreheads were pressed together, and he used his tongue to separate my lips. At first, I pulled back. I looked out of my peripheral vision, Selena and Keni were fingering each other. I pressed my lips to his as my nut gushed out of me.

"Damn dawg, you surprised the fuck outta me," Tyree said.

I smirked and said, "Shit me too."

"Y'all ready to get fucked?" Tyree asked the ladies.

They both eagerly nodded their heads. In my mind, I was strolling to the bed, but in actuality, I ran to that muthafucka. I leaned down to kiss Selena. We had a nasty, sloppy kiss. She spit in her hand and started jacking me off. We watched as Keni went down on Tyree. Selena used her other hand to slide her fingers inside Keni's pussy.

"This shit is so hot," I whispered.

"Fuck I'm about to cum, baby!" Ty yelled.

A few seconds later, he came all over Keni's face. She smiled, then leaned over and kissed Selena. I'm not sure if this afternoon could get any nastier. My wife pulled me onto the bed and told me to lay flat on my back.

Then she looked over at Keni and said, "Ride him good,

girl."

Shock was plastered on my face. I couldn't believe I was getting ready to fuck Keni. I wanted to know what her pussy felt like since forever. I was trying to hide my smile when she squatted over my hard dick. My eyes rolled to the back of my head when her silky walls wrapped around my length.

"Damn, Marcus," Keni moaned.

Tyree and Selena looked on in excitement.

"Ride that dick, good girl," Selena encouraged.

Selena laid on her back, and Tyree pushed her legs back and started eating her pussy. I focused on what Keni and I had going on. I looked up at her and smiled as my dick hit every curve.

"This pussy feels so good, baby," I moaned.

"This dick feels so good," she moaned back.

She wined her hips in a figure-eight motion and toyed with her nipples. I looked over to the other side of the bed to see what Ty and Selena were doing. She had her legs pushed back while he was sliding in and out of her.

He smacked Keni's ass and said, "Yeah, baby, ride that dick. I love to see that shit."

Our fucking was like music to my ears. I had never experienced something so blissful.

"Oh my god! Ty, you feel so good inside of me. Marcus baby," Selena moaned.

"That pussy feel good, doesn't it?" she asked.

"Hell yeah," I sighed.

I don't know how but shit got nastier. I continued to fuck

Keni and Tyree continued to fuck Selena. Keni leaned over to kiss Tyree. While I played with Selena's clit. Before I could bust my nut, Keni got up and sat on my face. I felt Selena sit on my dick, and she started riding me all wild and crazy. Tyree laid in between my legs and licked my balls while eating Selena out. We were all moaning, yelling, and cussing.

"Your tongue feels so good, Marcus," Keni groaned.

"This pussy taste good," I moaned into her crotch.

Selena had her back facing me, and she leaned into me and started eating Keni out. We were going at it like wild animals. Tyree crawled up to us, pushed Selena's knees to her chest, and slid into her pussy while I was still inside her.

"Fuck! Ooohh y'all fucking me so good!" She growled.

Between having Keni's pussy on my tongue, my wife's tight pussy wrapped around me, and my balls smacking against Tyree's, I was trying my hardest to hold my nut back.

"I'm about to cum y'all," Tyree said.

Everybody kept moaning. It felt like time had stood still; we all nutted at the same time. Tyree and I both nutted on Selena's stomach, Keni came on our faces, and Selena had creamed on our dicks.

"That was some good shit," Tyree said.

"Yes, it was. I've missed y'all," Keni said.

Selena and I were speechless. This was an experience we would never forget.

End of the trip...

Selena and I were cuddled up in the back seat as we headed to the airport. We all fucked two more times before leaving, and the shit felt better each time. Outside of the sex, we all promised to stay in touch.

I must admit that in some weird way, that foursome helped my marriage. Selena and I were freakier than ever. I don't know about us being swingers or having an open marriage, but it wouldn't hurt to fuck our friends every once in a while.

Nympho 20

F. A. N.

I'm a Man. I'm a dog, a pussy hound, a certified freak nigga! I say this with pride; I love pussy. All types of pussy, especially black pussy. I love the way it looks, the way it smells before and after a good fucking, the way it tastes, and how it talks while it's being fucked. I love pussy! But there was one thing I loved little more than pussy, and that was having a bitch's titties pressed against my back as she fucked me with a strap-on.

Yeah, you read that right, I loved having my asshole played with. Whether it was being fingered, fucked, or being licked, I loved all that shit. Depending on the woman, that was something I didn't disclose often. Not too many women were opened-minded about playing with a nigga's booty. They'd automatically assume that I was gay or some shit. I'll admit... when I've told women that I like anal play, rightfully so, they're shocked. I'm 6'6", bald head, wrapped in nothing but muscle. It's a mind game to know that a big nigga like myself loves a lil' back-door action.

I was 20 years old, and I was messing with this cougar. She was freaky on another level, always willing to try some new shit. One night, we were chilling at her place, and she was giving me some slow, sloppy head. She was massaging my balls. Her tongue snaked towards my gooch. At that point, my eyes crossed because the shit was feeling good. I didn't even realize she had started licking my asshole.

"Can I slide a finger in you?" She asked, putting my dick back in her mouth.

I was so caught up in the moment that I didn't realize what she was asking me.

"Yeah," I quivered.

She slid her finger in my ass and jacked me off at the same time. That shit was so indescribable. It felt like my soul left my body. Two minutes later, I was busting a huge nut all over her face and sheets. Since then, I always tried to make ass play a requirement, but a nigga respected other people's boundaries.

∞∞∞

Pre-cum oozed from my tip as I thought back to that moment. My dick became more rigid. "Aye, suck this dick," I said to my lil' freak Karmen. I fucked with her heavy because she was down to try anything. I watched as she stroked the long plastic dick that wrapped around her thick hips and pelvis.

"After I fuck that chocolate ass real, good. I want you to bust your nut deep in my pussy," she said.

I smiled and told her, "I got you."

I laid flat on my back so she could straddle my face, and my dick was aligned perfectly with her mouth. Her spit slide down the sides of my shaft and I lifted my head higher and inhaled her scent. Her smell drove me crazy. I stuck my tongue out and flicked it across her engorged clit; before dipping it in her sweet hole. My toes curled when she licked the tip of my dick and started sucking on it.

"Yeah, baby, suck that dick," I mumbled.

I palmed both her ass cheeks like they were basketballs so that I could tongue fuck her pussy deeper.

"Ooohh shit nigga," she moaned.

My long tongue slithered its way to her pretty asshole. I circled it with my tongue, then snaked its way up and down Karmen's crack. I kissed and bit on her cheeks and smacked them. I stuck my tongue in her hole.

"Fuck 'Twon, that feels so good!" She yelled, cradling my head.

I was eating her so good; she had to stop sucking my dick. I lifted her out of 69 and had her chest lying flat on the bed. Now I could alternate between eating and licking both holes. I was going crazy feasting on her. Spit was sliding between her ass and pussy. My tongue traded places with my index and middle fingers.

"You like when daddy eat that pussy and ass baby?" I asked, making my fingers go deeper.

"Yes, daddy! Yes, nigga! I love it!" she yelled.

I continued to work my fingers in and out of her and kissed all over her thighs and cheeks.

"Oh, my Gawd! 'Twon, I'm about to cum, yes, make me cum all over your fingers," she moaned.

I slowly pulled my fingers out of her and sucked off her sweet cream.

"Whew, nigga you are about to get it. Lay on your back and hold your legs up," she demanded.

I happily obliged and held my legs up in the crook of my arm. She smacked my ass and used her free hand to jack off her strap-on. I could feel my dick getting harder. Karmen stuck her tongue out and let a thick stream of spit slide down the crack of my ass. She bent down and pushed my legs back further. I felt her warm tongue lick around my hole.

"Yeah, baby, eat this chocolate ass," I moaned.

Man, this girl knew how to drive a nigga crazy. She popped my balls in her mouth and jacked my dick off at the same time. Then she switched to eating my ass.

"This ass tastes so good, daddy," she said.

She slid her middle finger into my puckering hole.

"You ready for mamí to give you this dick? You want me to fuck that tight hole nigga?" she asked.

I smiled. Her talking shit made my dick even harder.

"Yeah, c'mon and fuck this booty girl," I moaned.

I handed her the lube off the nightstand and excitedly watched as she put a generous amount on the strap. Then squirted a glob in between my cheeks. She started to guide the strap inside. First, she worked it in nice and slow, until all of it was in me.

"Fuck, Karmen!" I yelled.

My eyes immediately rolled to the top of my head. She smiled as she slowly stroked me. My ass started pulsating around the plastic dick.

"You got some good ass, daddy," Karmen said.

She leaned down to kiss me. I grabbed onto her waist to help guide her movements. She leaned up, pushed my hands away.

She said, "I got this nigga, this ain't my first time fucking you."

"Then quit playing and fuck me," I groaned.

She slowly started to speed up. I could feel her sweet juices slid down my crack. Her strokes made pre-cum leak from my dickhead, and she began to drill my ass.

"I love fucking this chocolate ass nigga. It's so wet and tight," she moaned.

"Yeah, this booty all yours, Karmen."

"That's what I like to hear, daddy."

She continued to fuck me good, hard, and fast. I jacked my dick off to the rhythm of her fucking. I bit down on my bottom lip. She spit, on my dick, and took my place jacking off, doing this little twist and up & down combo.

"C'mon, Karmen fuck this ass boo. I ain't no bitch," I moaned.

She gave me exactly what I wanted. She was stroking my ass hard and fast.

"That's how you like it, 'Twon. You like when bitches fucking this pretty hole? Tell me you like being slutted out?" She asked.

"I love being bitched out!" I yelled.

She fucked me harder, and began hitting my porstate, causing my legs to shake. Pussy juice started leaked on my ass. I reached underneath me and played in her wetness.

"Ooohh, you know I love when you do that, Antwon," she moaned.

I smiled. I could feel my balls tighten and a tingle in the tip of my dick.

"Fuck girl, you about to make me nut!" I yelled.

"Unt unh, save that gooey nut for my pussy. You got me so wet right now."

She fucked harder, and my asshole started to tighten around the strap-on.

"'Twon finger me, harder daddy!" She yelled.

I worked my fingers harder; right when I felt my nut about to spill out of me, she pulled out and smacked my hole. She leaned down and started eating me out. Her tongue felt so good. My hole kept opening and closing. Once I had enough, I stood up on my feet, picked her up, and threw her on the bed.

"You about to get this dick Karm," I said, stroking my pipe.

She took the strap off and threw it across the room. She opened her legs wide and started playing with herself. My pipe was so hard; it bounced up and down by itself.

"Come and fuck me, 'Twon," she said.

I finally climbed on the bed, pushed her legs back, and spit on her cunt before sliding in. Once I was in, that thang started talking. Her juices soaked my balls. Her moaning and groaning made me pump faster and harder.

"This pussy so good and wet. I can't wait to nut in it," I moaned.

"Yeah, I want you to nut so deep in me," she moaned back.

I leaned down to suck on her nipples and kiss her. She held me tight as I glided in and out.

"Fuck! Shit! I'm right there, boo I feel it I'm about to bust!"

I yelled.

Karmen had already cum about three or four times. Her cream had my dick coated. When she started playing with my nipples, I knew it wasn't long before my orgasm washed over me. I quit long stroking and started pumping.

"Fuck yeah, baby! I feel it. I'm about to bust all up in yo' shit!" I yelled.

I felt like I was bussing buckets of cum. I smacked my pelvis into hers going deeper and finally releasing inside of her warm, wet walls.

"Oh, my Gawd! Nigga you feel so good cumming inside me," she moaned.

I held her legs open and said, "Push that nut out."

I watched as she pushed my nut from her pussy. I loved when our juices mingled together. I leaned down because I couldn't help but taste the fruits of our labor. My tongue snaked between her ass and pussy. I was trying to lick up as much of our love as possible. Her nails grazed my bald head.

"I wanna taste daddy."

I leaned over her, with our nut in my beard, and smothered all around my face. She greedily sucked on my tongue.

"'Twon, that was so good, but next time I wanna invite a friend," she said.

I laid on my back, trying to catch my breath, and said, "Whatever you want, baby."

Acknowledgements

First and foremost, I would like to thank the most high, the creator, and the universe for blessing with this wonderful talent. About 13 years ago, I made a promise to myself that I would be a published author and a New York Times Bestselling Author. My dream is finally coming true. I couldn't have made this happen by myself, the support from my family and friends has been what's kept me motivated. There have been numerous times when I wanted to give up, but it was my family & friends that kept me prayed up with their support. I love every single person, that has ever read my stories and have graced me with their feedback.

I have a few people I would like to thank, First I want to thank my parents and siblings for constantly being my support system and always encouraging me to take that leap of faith. Without y'all none of this would be possible. Second, I want to thank all of my friends who have waited patiently for years, for me to finally publish my book. I wish I could name all of y'all but its too many to count, but know that your love and support of me has not gone unnoticed and has always been greatly appreciated. Lastly, I would like to thank GraphicGoons/Morii Owens, for exceeding my expectations with this cover. You really did that!

This isn't the end, this is just the beginning. I am excited to see where this journey takes me, because it has been a long time coming. For anyone having a hard time trying to take a leap of faith or wanting to follow their dreams, all I can say is just do it! Sometimes it isn't the world that holds us back, but our own fears of failing that hold us back. Don't be afraid to show your talents and gifts with the world, you may never know who you are helping out of hard time.

As always I wish Love, Peace, Happiness, and Abundance on all of my loved ones.

-Love, Ka'mooRe.

Made in the USA
Monee, IL
14 October 2021